C. Hankins has always loved reading and [illegible] her schooling years, she struggled with writing, and her English tutors would point this out to her. Still, that did not stop her from making up stories and writing them at home, especially at a younger age. She felt more at ease because she was not being criticised or judged for the structure/grammar. At the age of 9 or 10, her love for writing in her diary began, and most evenings, she would reflect on her day and write about it. Christiana loved recounting and sharing her thoughts, sometimes expressing what she couldn't convey to others in writing.

As she grew older, she also fell in love with journaling and writing about everything: songs, poems, words of encouragement, testimonies/gratitude, and so forth. Once Christiana started writing about things, it could be endless, spending hours doing so. It's a desire and passion that has permanently been embedded within her soul, that she finds hard to explain. Although, born in Sierra Leone, Christiana's home is still in the UK, where she has spent most of her life growing up. She loves travelling, and she is blessed to be in a profession that does not limit but enhances her passion further.

For my dearest Charlotte Therese Purser, who I call mommy Charl and cousin. Thank you for your constant listening ears, warmest hugging arms, and forever reassuring words of encouragement and guidance during my stages of growth.

C. Hankins

The Unexpected Matters of the Heart

Austin Macauley Publishers™
London • Cambridge • New York • Sharjah

A CIP catalogue record for this title is available from the British Library.

ISBN 9781035823499 (Paperback)
ISBN 9781035823512 (ePub e-book)
ISBN 9781035823505 (Audiobook)

www.austinmacauley.co.uk

First Published 2024
Austin Macauley Publishers Ltd®
1 Canada Square
Canary Wharf
London
E14 5AA

To my friends and family, thank you for all you do and will continue to do. Your inspiration is what brought these characters to life. Once again, thank you to the Austin Macauley team for your dedication and support throughout the publication process.

Table of Contents

Chapter 1
Setting the Background and Scene

Can you believe it? Two weeks have indeed flown by. Well, let's just say, the first week because during the second week, time seemed to have frozen with each passing day. Finally, I was out of quarantine! Two weeks' worth of quarantine in the same room. I mean, to some, this was a dream come true. No disturbances from the busy world or nosey people who seem always to want to be in your business.

But to me, ugh…no way. The concept of rest was far from me. Two weeks prior, I had just flown from the UK in a journey that was even crazy to tell. I mean, how I got onto that flight was a divine connection. My faith played a crucial role in making it possible.

So yeah, quarantine, goodbye to you. May we never meet again, either in this life or the next. Stay away from me and my front door forever.

As I stood with my two big luggage, hand luggage and handbag, I tightly held on to the official release documents with my dear life. I just wanted to reach the apartment. This will be a place I hope to make into a home. I wonder what the apartment will be like.

I surely hope the pictures I saw previously were not deceiving. It had happened to me before in my last venture adventure. What a story to even tell. So now I'm extra sceptical when pictures are shown to me of places.

It's not like I was there when they took those pictures. For all I know, they could have gone and highjacked someone's lovely apartment. In the world we live in today, anything crazy is possible. It's the norm.

But anyway, I continued to stand and wait in anticipation for someone to collect me. I mean, come on, it's not like you found out an hour ago of my release day. It had been two days prior. Not much of a difference to some, but to me, of course. Remember, each passing day in quarantine was like forever.

Waiting now is something I was really not enjoying but many questions pondered against my mind on this whole experience for the last two weeks. But the number one question at this current time was, 'where are the people who were supposed to pick me?'

To be honest, if I had an enemy and wanted them to be irritated, I would definitely recommend them to experience quarantine and then go through the motion of waiting for some more time to be picked up in a location you have no clue about the whereabouts.

'Beep, beep, beep', the horns went, interrupting me from my endless thoughts. Finally, they have arrived to pick me up. The journey to my new apartment was one of a kind. I know people say these things to show something happened and they don't want to talk about it. Yet, I say this out: I have no clue of my surrounding, and thank goodness, I'm a free woman.

Not long after arriving at my new home, yes I called it that (despite I hadn't yet unpacked fully or made it homely). I had to shoot back out to sort out my new phone, SIM card and eat something since, after all, the last 14 days I've been deprived of what I had desired to eat.

Evening came, and I was getting ready to hit the town. No, it's not what you're thinking. I was invited to the KTV experience by a friend of a friend. I know right, it hasn't even been 24 hours and I'm already making friends. Well, my close friend, who was here previously and recommended me the job, had a friend who was still here, so she had invited me.

Let's just say the evening was eventful even though I am yet to unpack, but at least I have the weekend and the week ahead, since there was a school break that awaited me. Lucky me, hey.

Chapter 2
The Unexpected Encounter: Games Night

Sunday crept in on me in no time. Games night was another invitation from my friend's friend, Dee. Well, I didn't hesitate to say yes because anything to do with games has me hooked. Evening came, and we set out to the game night host at his house. The same area where we live but a different building. Better early than late.

Since Dee and I were the first ones there, I soon started to feel comfortable even though I was a bit shy. I know right, who can imagine me being shy? I started helping Rhy in the kitchen as he prepared food for us, when the doorbell suddenly went.

So me being me, I decided to go and open it, pretending it was my home. Only heaven knows what Rhy was thinking. Without hesitation, I went to open the door. "Welcome to my…"

Well, well, well, who has my eyes bestowed upon? If time could stop, this would surely be the moment I would like time to stop. Why wasn't there a camera around to capture this moment? Destiny has indeed met because who did I open the door to?

Well, it was an unexpected individual. An eye candy that made my heart smile. What? How was this possible? It has been too long since my heartfelt this way, but I refuse to fall into the circle of the past. But why is my heart now doing skips? Does it need a doctor's check? I was stunned.

After a moment that felt forever, I decided to let him in and introduce myself. What did he say his name is because I'm blown away right now and couldn't hear what he had said? *Okay, keep it together*, I told myself. *You just met him. You can't be head over heels for this guy you just met.*

But then again, mmm. The war in me has now begun. *Just be natural*, I say to myself as I take a deep breath. I went back to the kitchen to help Rhy and try to calm my thoughts that were blasting within me of why destiny is only making us just meet now. Where has this eye candy been all my life? The endless questions continued within me.

As the night went on, two other people came, and yes, one was Dat. Where do I start with him? With a few words as possible, we can just say he is an interesting character who can't help but flirt. Don't get me wrong, he is also an attractive tall guy with charisma, but he is no eye candy.

Dat decided to add my WeChat account, and since I was intrigued, I decided to accept his request. But like I said, he is not eye candy. He should have entered before him and maybe (more like a slight slim hope) been almost an eye candy.

The night continued, and flirting was happening between Dat and myself. Still, I was in deep thoughts over eye candy, whose eyes were also deep in thought like mine. Luckily, an opportunity arose during one of the games for everyone to say a bit about themselves; I was delighted because now I could find out a bit about eye candy. I mean, at least his name.

He looks so mysterious. So much he seems to be holding back, and to be honest, I was trying not to stare, but my staring did me no good. Anyway, I distracted myself and just kept my head in the game. During the rest of the night, no words were exchanged between myself and eye-candy. Neither were there any stares swapped.

Time swept away, and in no time, we had to leave. I can only imagine when our path will once again cross.

Chapter 3
A Swift in Time: Fast-Forward

Oh my goodness, where did the time pass so fast. I can't believe I am back to the working routine. Okay, I can do this. I've had such an eventful week off during the Golden holidays, but the concept of rest wasn't entirely on my agenda.

Work finally began, and the first week was such a drag, and when I mean it dragged, even a snail was faster. After all, we started on a Saturday and only had one day off. What a bummer.

As I walked on the school ground, I could see someone familiar in the distance. Oh, to my surprise, that's eye candy I can see. "Hiya," I waved. But no response. What's with the sudden coldness? Weren't we in the same company the other week? Don't you remember me?

I mean, come on, my hairstyle is still the same, and dare I say, so is my smile. A deep sigh aroused within me as he barely waved back at me. Anyways, no offence taken.

The weeks continued to pass me by, and I barely saw him, and the times I did see him, no conversation was exchanged between us. What's his problem? Did I do something to him in the previous life?

The days continued to pass by and the work-life balance was far from me. An emotional wreck is what I've been experiencing lately. I've been feeling so exhausted, and now I wish I had truly rested in quarantine and the Golden holiday.

Another long day at work and now I'm off to get the bus back home. After finding a random seat, hold and behold who got on the bus; it's him. What's his name again? Why am I so terrible at remembering? Well, after all, it is not like he has noticed me.

I barely said hello but gently smiled at him as his eyes wandered on where he should sit. As destiny will once again have it, the only available seat nearby was the one in front of me.

During the journey, I couldn't help but stare at his hair. My goodness, talk about fine, smooth hair. Withholding my need to stroke the back of his hair, I quickly started humming to take my mind off him.

Halting, the bus, came to our stop, and thankfully, he had his earphones on throughout the journey. As quick as lightning, he hurried off the bus. Only heaven knows his problem.

Another staff meeting was held at work. What a long day. The last place I would like to be was in a long meeting. If there was an option for me concerning this meeting, I surely know what mine will be.

As the meeting went on, I couldn't stop thinking of my new hairstyle. You see, I had rushed while making it over the weekend. Now I'm conscious of what others are thinking. It's all in my head, I know, but I hate when I do a hairstyle, and I'm not sure of it.

In fact, the extension style was beautiful, but it wasn't enough on my head, so I had to make it work. Oh God, please help me rock this hair till next week, and I will take it off. "Sarah, Sarah, the meeting is finished," a voice said. Wow, so lost in my deep thoughts once again that I didn't realise how quickly the time had gone by.

Now have to put this chair away and head back to my classroom. As I stood up to take my chair back to the other side of the room, hold and behold who walked towards me. Someone I didn't expect. Why is he coming towards me? How am I looking? Oh great.

Act natural, Sarah. Don't let your nerves show on your face. You've got this. You've got this. You've... "Your hair looks nice," echoed the words out of his mouth. Not just any mouth but eye candy's mouth.

"Thank you," I repeated back with a smile.

As quickly as those words were echoed out, that's how fast he walked off away from me. What just happened? Am I dreaming? Hello, can someone please pinch me? Where am I now? What was I about to do? All these questions flooded my mind as I stared at my chair.

"Sarah, Sarah, are you going back to your classroom?" Another voice said. Oh, reality just has to kick in again quickly. *Back to earth, girl,* I told myself. Okay, off I return my chair and head off to my classroom. Nearly home time. What a day. Undoubtedly, grateful that is over.

Several weeks swing by and it's already the first week in December. What? Where are the months flying by? But at least, soon it will be the winter break.

Today was finally the day I picked up my parcels from Taoboa order. I've meant to go to the delivery section but I've been so busy. It's been almost a week of procrastination. But today, after work, I intend to. I mean, it is only 5 minutes from where I live, next to where the school bus drops us off.

The day ended and I went to catch the bus with some of my friends. Now, where should we sit? Here looks like a good seat. Hopefully, this journey goes fast. Tonight was also the night I told Dani we could make pancakes together.

But have I got the strawberries and blueberries we needed? Nope; work has kept me busy to even organise myself like that. It's okay. After the bus stops, I will quickly run to the fruit market before picking up my parcels.

As I go through the plan in my head, guess who walks on the bus. EYE CANDY. He quickly took a seat somewhere after his eyes scrounger back and forth. I don't really care. I don't know his problem. Honestly, his split personality is annoying me. But then again, damn you and your physics.

Anyway, the bus ride couldn't have gone quicker. Upon arriving at the bus stop near our home, the ladies asked me if I needed help collecting my parcels. "Mmm, I think I will be fine," I told them.

"Are you sure, Sarah?" They said.

"Well," I said. "On a second note, I think I will need your help as I don't want to risk it. But, ladies, I first need to go to the fruit store if that's okay."

After they agreed, we walked there. Hold and behold who we encountered in the same store. EYE CANDY again. Why is he following me, or does it look like I'm following him? This is not a cat and mouse chasing game—just plain coincidence.

Still, as I saw him, I started acting naturally. But wasn't I acting natural already. Now, I'm confused. Why is he so good at confusing my mind without even knowing it? Okay, Sarah, focus. "I'm on a mission," I told myself quietly.

"What is it I needed again?" My friends asked me.

Errrr, even I'm asking the same question. *Sarah, think fast. Don't be head over heels again.* I remembered finally and snapped at myself. "Strawberries and blueberries," I said. So we found the strawberries. "But where are the blueberries?" I uttered out loud.

"They are over here," a voice responded. Not just any voice but eye candy's voice.

"Thanks," I answered. Now time to pay and head to the place to collect my parcels. It's no time for any distractions.

At the payment counter, the cashier spoke to me and smiled away. If only he knew I neither knew nor spoke Chinese, he wouldn't have troubled himself to try. I just smiled at him as I paid. Off us ladies went to get the parcels, leaving eye candy in the store.

Now, we finally arrived at the place to collect the parcels. I felt so tired as we stood there waiting for the assistant to give me all my packages. But I'm not allowed to be tired. I still have pancakes that await me with Dani.

One by one, the guy kept on bringing boxes after boxes. What? How is it possible I ordered so many Christmas things? The boxes were so much that the guy offered his delivery cart to help carry some of the packages. The ladies just looked at me and laughed.

Honestly, if they had not insisted on helping me, I don't know what I would have done. Each of them held two of the items while I attempted to push the cart with tons of boxes that kept on falling off. *Why me?* I asked myself silently. After this Christmas season is over, I tell you, no more big shopping like this for me from Taoboa online.

We approached the entrance gate and I told Dani to give us the things she was carrying as she needed to get almond milk from her building to make the pancakes. I was short of almond milk and hadn't had time to order some. To be honest, it didn't make sense for her to make a double trip to my building, then hers and mine again.

As Simmy and I continued, I couldn't take it anymore with these stupid boxes falling down. "Good God, please help us," I whispered to myself. Before I could finish saying that, hold and behold once again, I saw eye candy emerging through the entrance gate, and what happened next, only God could help me.

My mouth ran faster than my brain. I began to shout his name. With a freight, he looked my way. "Please, come here," I continued to call. I mean, at this point in time, this poor confused guy was either frightened or shocked at how loudly I was shouting his name to come to where I was. Soon, the whole neighbourhood will know his name.

But I have no remorse because these boxes were frustrating life out me, and my prayer was strangely answered. As he approached me, I didn't know what had taken over because what happened next was also unbelievable. "Please help me; give me your things," I said, as I grabbed it from his hands. "Here you go, please push this cart," I also said, and began to walk away with his things and left him with my boxes on the carts.

Poor guy. I know he didn't sign up for this, but I had to be bossy otherwise I would still be suffering with Simmy, who was as shocked and confused as him on what was happening.

As we continued walking to my building, I laughed, and Simmy and eye candy continued to make conversations on how come I was carrying light and easy things which weren't mine, while they were suffering with my things.

I kept reassuring them I was thankful and happy, even though I was laughing. As we made our way into my building and the lift (on the 10th floor), I was still in disbelief at what was happening. Simmy started teasing me in the elevator that I should treat both her and eye candy after suffering with my many things and then asked him his thoughts on a good place to eat.

"Chilli's," he responded and spoke a bit more.

"What?" Simmy replied, "We should make her take us somewhere expensive."

"Simmy," I interrupted, "be kind and don't give him the wrong idea." Upon arriving at my front door, he started offloading the things at the front door. "You can bring them inside," I said, and with no hesitation, he did. While Simmy used the restroom, I kept on saying thank you to him and how grateful I was.

As they both were leaving, he then said, "Would you like me to take the cart back for you?"

In shock, I blurted out, "Really?" Today must be pre-Christmas for me, I thought. *Okay, Sarah, compose yourself.* "Really?" I said once again, sounding confusing like the first time I said it. "You don't have to."

"I don't mind; it's only at the front gate," he responded.

"But, this is from the other side where the parcels can be delivered at no.66," I interrupted.

"That's quite far and I'm not that nice," he said as he chuckled.

"I understand," I responded. "It will be too far for you. Don't worry, I will take it back tomorrow."

In no time, they both left, leaving me blown away from the whole experience of what just happened.

The evening continued with Simmy now joining Dani and me for the pancake night. Both girls couldn't stop laughing and teased me about the experience of what had previously happened. In fact, I couldn't blame them because if I was in their shoes, I would definitely be doing so. Nice of me, hey.

As the evening carried on, I decided to message eye candy, inviting him to join us for pancake night as an appreciation. 'Hey, I can't thank you enough for your help. The girls and I are making pancakes. If you would like, you can join us'.

In no time, he messaged back. 'You're welcome. That's very kind of you, but I will give it a pass this time. I just ate dinner'.

'Well', I said, 'I'm still bringing you some over'.

'You don't have to', he then said.

'I want to', I replied. 'You don't have a choice. I'm still bringing it over; after all, it's the least I could do'.

'Okay, since you insist', he responded.

'Good', I said. 'What building and floor do you live at?'…and so the messages went on.

As the girls were leaving, I left with them, holding eye candy's pancakes in one container, strawberries and blueberries in another, and chocolate spread tin. I mean, who can't be tempted with chocolate spread, especially hazelnut. I absolutely love it on pancakes and hope he does too. As I got in the lift, I tried to be as natural as a summer day, even though this very situation is not at all-natural. Far off from natural.

The doors pulled apart as I stepped out of the lift. I scanned across the doors until my eyes are fixed on his. Knock, knock, knock, I gently went on his door. No answer. *Mmm, I hope I'm at the right door*, I thought to myself. As I returned to his messages to confirm the door number, I heard footsteps. "Hi," came a voice as the door opened.

"Hi, this is for you," I quickly said.

"Awww, you didn't have to. You're too kind," he said.

Suddenly, I couldn't respond. What happened to my voice? Why, all of a sudden, I'm struggling to speak up. Voice, hello. This is not the time you should be on holiday. Now this silence from me that I didn't want.

"Let me give you back your containers as I'm terrible at returning them," he said as he made his way to the kitchen and broke the silence of my no response.

"Really," I echoed silently from my mouth as I invited myself into his home and followed him to the kitchen, leaving the door wide open. "I also brought chocolate spread for you," I silently spoke again.

"Thank you, but I already have some," he said. "Oh, that's why you were buying strawberries and blueberries earlier," he said as he noticed the container with them.

"Yeah," I replied. "Well, I will leave you to it. Thank you once again," I murmur, and at the speed of lightning, I left his apartment with the chocolate spread tin and plate that had the pancakes. As for the container with the fruits, I'm sure he will give it to me once he is done.

I couldn't stop thinking what an interesting evening it had been as I walked away. I continued to ponder as I took each step, replaying all the actions and conversations that had happened in my head. But wait a minute, voice, how could you have let me down like that and made me unable to speak properly earlier.

Anyway, that's a digging investigation for another day. Work is in the morning, and another parcel has arrived for me to collect at another collection area, but luckily, it is across from the entrance gate.

The December weeks were starting to go fast, and only a few times did I see eye candy around work, but this guy became unbelievable again. It's like we had never met or never had an almost special moment taking place between us. One evening was the last straw for me.

I was walking to pick up a parcel and he was walking from picking up his. Let's just say I was getting ready to say hello, and this guy walked past me like he didn't see me. I was shocked. He was literally in his own world like nothing else existed around him.

Hello, who do you think you are? I know you're tall and I'm pretty short, but you're not a giant, and I'm not a midget for you not to see me. And it doesn't matter, that it was evening and a bit dark. Are you telling me I'm invisible to be seen by your eyes?

This situation bothered me. Right! Two can play that game. I'm also going to ignore you. Two can also have split personalities. I don't care how much I like you, but I can't stand rudeness and snob people.

Over a week went by, and one of my dear close friends came to spend Christmas with me, especially as her school had the actual time off. One Saturday morning, Tee and I embarked on an IKEA journey for Christmas and home shopping. Not like I haven't already received tons of parcels of Christmas decorations. Well, more was needed in my eyes.

It was a well-spent day filled with laughter, food, and unity. On our way back to the flat and being astonished at how people can spend so much on home things, that person being myself, of course, I realised I had bought a table display. Oh dear, I had no tools to fix it. How can I fix this? What do I do, and whom should I ask?

Oh no, a crazy idea just popped into my head. I wonder if I could message eye candy and if he would allow me to borrow his tools. I will definitely give it a go on fixing the table. Okay, here I go. The worse he could say his no to me borrowing his tools, and then I will think of plan b.

'Hey, do you have tools by any chance?' I messaged. And now the wait begins for me. To my surprise, a message came through from him not long after. 'Yeah, what do you need doing', he said.

So I responded, 'Just an IKEA table & pictures'.

'Okay, I could come and fix it tomorrow', he says.

Huh? Did my eyes just read correctly? Did he just volunteer to fix my table? Did I ask him to do it? Let me just scan through the conversation to make sure I hadn't. No sign I did. "Tee, please read this conversation because I'm confused and don't know if I'm reading things wrong."

As I passed Tee my phone, I was still shocked. "No, my friend, your brain is not playing upon you. He volunteered himself," she says.

What a relief, I thought. 'Yes, tomorrow is good with me', I then responded to him before he started thinking I was as rude as him.

'Yeah, sure, I could come round at 5 pm?' he then said.

Mmm, 5 won't be good for me, I ponder in my thoughts. I have church in the morning, then spend the day with Tee and baking with Tee and Dani. Now I have to squeeze in another activity. But if I don't take tomorrow, I'm stranded with my IKEA table unfixed. Okay, maybe I could cheekily see if around 6-ish pm is possible for him. So I responded by asking him that time as I was occupied during the day.

'Okay, I will message you then', he says.

Wow, has this guy changed a new leaf. I'm shocked. Just like that, he agreed. Has Christmas indeed come early? I know it's only about a week to go. Technically, it's only next Friday. So I responded with thank you, and he is the best.

Now all I have to do is make sure I'm done with all the activities and be home with Tee by 6.30 pm. Surely, that's not a bad thing unless something else springs up, I wonder.

As church service went on the following day, my mind could not be far from distracted. Hello mind, focus. Listen to the teaching. Stop wandering once again on eye candy. After service, Tee and I enjoyed our shopping and exploring time at the mall.

We then went for late lunch at Texas Roadhouse to put the icing on the day. My goodness, they have the best fresh bread with cinnamon butter. Honestly, I could snack on that and be full. And that was pretty much what happened.

Time swung by and we soon took the Didi taxi home. Okay, what's the time? 3.45 pm. Right, we need to head over to Dani for baking. So far, so good on time.

Poor Tee, if only she knew what she signed up for by agreeing to spend time with me during this holiday. "Tee, are you okay? I'm sorry once again on our busy schedule," I said.

"No, girl, it's fine, you don't need to say sorry," she warmly said with a smile. Eish, thank God for having such an understanding friend. The time at Dani was enjoyable but went slowly, and honestly, I couldn't stop staring at my phone every so often.

"Has he messaged?" Tee asked.

With shaking of the head, I responded, "Nope." It's 6.15 pm already and still nothing from him. Either way, we will still head home, just in case he turns up. Feeling guiltier to drag Tee and shoot off from Dani's, we speed walk to my building. Okay, it's 6.30 pm and we barely made it back to the flat.

Tick tock tick tock, still no sign of him or a message. I hope he hasn't been kidnapped as it's now 6.50 pm. Right, I'm going to give him 15 minutes, and if I don't hear from him, I'm sending a message. *What is this?* I thought to myself.

This guy will not make me go crazy by considering what could have happened to him. After all, he volunteered, so he needs to keep his word even though he doesn't owe me anything. But still.

Well, it's now 7.10 pm, so I sent a message.

'Hiya…just checking if you are still coming?'

'Hey! I literally just got back. You ok for me to head over now? Which building you in?' he replied.

'Oh dear…sorry, I didn't know you were out. Of course, you can if you aren't tired, I'm in building…'

'What is it that needs to be fixed exactly? Ha-ha. Take a pic of it', he responded.

So I did, and in my head, I wasn't going to make him postpone. There was no way; I rushed and rearranged my Sunday for him to chicken out of coming to fix my display table. Nope, I'm not taking no as an answer.

'Ah, I see. I can help you with that', he said.

'Awesome. See you soonish', I respond.

‘What’s your evening like tomorrow? Shall I come tomorrow instead? I think it’ll take a while’, another message came from him.

What? Is this guy having a laugh? Nope, by fire by force, this brother bear is coming tonight. I’m not going to rearrange another day for him. Does he think I haven’t got anything better to do with my life but sit around and wait for him? I don’t think so.

So I responded, ‘I’m sorry, already busy decorating Christmas cookies with the girls tomorrow’, with a crying emoji.

Then he wrote, ‘Ok, let me come over and sort out your IKEA desk first at least then’.

Yes, that did the trick. Good old women cry and emotions. It hasn’t let us down before, and I’m sure in the 100 years to come, it won’t either.

‘Awesome… you’re the best’, I responded.

Not long after, there was a knock on my door. I calmly opened the door, pretending I wasn’t relieved to have him over or my afternoon wasn’t shifted around for him. After introducing him to Tee, he started to work on my IKEA box.

Prior to today, Tee and I had set up a hot chocolate station, so I thought to myself, what better way to try it out but on him being my guest.

“You don’t mind almond milk, do you? That’s what I use and would like to make you a hot drink?” I said.

“No, don’t mind. Are you lacto?” He responded.

“Yes,” I answer back while nodding my head.

“Same here,” he echoed back.

“This is for you,” I said.

“Oh, you didn’t have to; you’re too kind,” he responded.

"Well, I said, it's the least I could do for stealing your precious time…"

As he carried on trying to make sense of the different pieces for the table, I began to strike a conversation with him. Well, I don't know where the courage came from, but the conversation became endless. We spoke about what we had been up to concerning this day, interests, what he planned to do during the winter break, how he was spending his Christmas Day, and so forth.

As the conversation was flowing and he was fixing the table shelf, I helped him and attempted to arrange his toolbox. Disappointing effort as nothing was staying in its place but he appreciated the thought.

I don't know how it happened, but one of the screws ended up going missing for the table, still; he indeed did improvisation.

At one moment, I forgot Tee was still around, who at the time was in the same room but on the phone to her family. As eye candy finished fixing the shelf table, the time was going, and I remembered work was tomorrow for both of us. Sipping almost the last of hot drink from the mug, he started admiring my balcony night view.

With the endless conversation I got lost in, I began to tour him around the flat. Only heaven knows what was in his mind, especially as my mouth wouldn't zip it. As we made our way to the final section unseen, my bedroom, I started talking about where I would like to hang the pictures on the wall.

I forgot that Tee had finished her family conversation for a while and she was also touring the flat with us. What a friend, hey.

Not long after that, he said his goodbye as he made his way through my front door with some biscuit snacks I made him take. I'm not helping him with his structure, and I even told him to send evidence of when he finishes the snacks. Poor guy; if only he knew how bossy I could be, he definitely would have run away a while ago.

Standing in the living room staring at Tee, she couldn't help but chuckle.

"Share, G, what's so funny?" I said.

"You two. The way you were to each other. Also, my mom and sis think he is a good catch," she responded.

"Huh, what do you mean?" I whispered back.

"Well, G, when I was on call to them, it was a video call and I faced the camera to you two. They were just admiring both of you on the floor together. Also, G, confession time, I videoed you two while you were touring him around the flat."

"Well," I say. "I'm sincerely gobsmacked. You should indeed work for the FBI because I had no clue what you were up to. On that note," my voice raised. "Let me see the video, girl…"

A couple of days went by and Tee and Simmy wanted to do Korean BBQ. I mean, who could say no to this. I absolutely love it.

"Mmm, I wonder if eye candy would like to join us," I said to them both.

"Why don't you find out," Simmy said. "After all, you, too, are basically friends now."

And so I thought. But after reaching out, this guy took his time to respond and said if I had asked him 10 minutes before, then it would have been fine, but he had already eaten. Am I a spy? How do I know your dinner time?

The excuses that flow from his mouth are like a running stream. I can't keep up. Anyway, who cares? I don't know why I thought we had passed the awkward barrier and now on a new leaf. I suppose we are now back to stage zero.

Oh well, I don't care anyway. It's your loss. After all, I was just trying to be nice.

Chapter 4
Surprise, Surprise

What? I can't believe it is Christmas Day already. Where have the last couple of months gone, and why so quick? In fact, not even the months but weeks, if I may say. Unfortunately, Joony cancelled last night coming over to spend Christmas Eve and Christmas Day with Tee and me, as she is not feeling well.

Tee and I had bought so much food to feed the whole army, which anyway was still yet to be cooked. Well, at least the desserts were made last night. My homemade traditional Christmas upside-down pineapple cake. A true classic throughout my Christmas memories of teenagerhood.

Now the tradition should live on even if I'm on the other side of the world, away from my family, who had been so used to indulging in the delicacies. It's a good thing I also invited Dani and her fiancé over for Christmas dinner. I hate to imagine Tee and me attempting to devour all these different foods.

Why did we get so many meats again? Oh, I remember, we are reliving the Middle Eastern days. This was not the first Christmas holiday Tee and I were spending together. A couple of years back, when our adventures were in Qatar and living together, we stayed there one Christmas and celebrated, if I may say, in style; what a spectacular Christmas to remember, if I may say so myself. I'm sure others around us then could genuinely testify to it too.

Christmas day was passing us by, and luckily, we had told Dani and her fiancée to come during the late afternoon. Since morning, Tee and I have been making dish after dish of delicious foods. With all the trying of the different dishes, will I have space in my stomach when it's time to eat? Well, after all, it is the season to be jolly, in my own words, jolly in the feast.

As the day passed us by, Dani arrived with her fiancé, and we all relaxed as we dined. With the amount of flavours dancing in my mouth, I have to give credit to Tee and myself for our well worth hard work. I'm sure our guests also agreed. As we were all relaxing and chilling, I couldn't stop and wondered how eye candy was doing on this day.

Mmm, what had he mentioned last week on how he was spending this day? What was it, I wonder? Oh yeah, he was spending his day being on phone calls to family around the world. Well, I doubt he would have taken time out to cook for himself. And besides, this is Christmas Day. Everyone should be enjoying a homemade cooked Christmas dinner dish.

Well, the next thing that happened, I couldn't believe it myself. So I first contemplated the idea a lot in my head. Should I, shouldn't I? What would he think, I wonder. But then again, there is so much food Tee and I made. It would be such a waste not to share.

I love sharing, especially with those I care about or for. So what, I don't mind if he thinks I'm crazy. I've made up my mind to share. So without question, I took a big, and when I said a big, I'm not joking. I took the most oversized plate I had and dished food for him.

Now, where is the container? He will need gravy, but just in case he doesn't like sauce, it's best it goes in the container. Mmm, well, dessert is also required, and since we made two types, he can enjoy them both.

I quickly excused myself from my guest, with Tee knowing what I was up to. After all, she is my close G, so she must share my ideas no matter how crazy they are.

As I walked over to his building, a thousand and one thoughts flooded my mind. I arrived in front of the building and the main door was closed. Oh, man. Now, if I buzz his apartment, he might not respond or be shy and refuse. What should I do now? Great, this idea that seemed crazily good is now going pear shape.

Hold on a minute; I can press the assistance buzzer. In each building, there is one, and it will open the building door. To be honest, he was the one that had previously taught me that. The same day I ambushed him to help me push my carts with tons of Christmas boxes on them, my main building door wouldn't open, so he told me about the assistance buzzer for each building.

I felt so silly for not previously knowing. Months back, whenever I had been out with friends and my main building door was closed, and my card won't let me in, I would walk back to the entrance gate in the cold to call the security guy to open it for me—all those times. A teardrop nearly fell from my eyes. Involuntary exercise I was doing. I felt a big sigh coming over me as I pondered those times.

I'm now in the lift, and I stare at myself through the glass mirror. "What are you doing you?" I asked myself. "Oh well,"

I quickly responded, “there is no turning back, I’m already in the lift and three stops from his floor. No turning back now.” I chuckled to myself. Only heaven knows what those who are watching the CCTV cameras are wondering, especially why this girl is talking and chuckling to herself.

As the lift door opened, my heart pounded furiously and my hands began to sweat. Why am I being nervous? Surely this is a normal thing, or have I convinced myself it is. No, indeed it is.

Knock, knock, knock, I gently went on his door. Again I repeated and still no response. What? Did I get it wrong? Surely I heard him clearly the other time. Didn’t he say he will be home Christmas Day on calls with family?

Maybe he didn’t say that. As the questions flooded my mind once again, I heard faint footsteps. Before I could raise my hand to knock again, the door handle turned and opened.

“Hiya,” I responded with a smile. “Merry Christmas.”

“I wasn’t quite sure if I could hear my door knocking. Once I’m in the bedroom locked, I struggle to hear my front door…”

“No worries,” I quickly responded. “I remembered you were saying you will be on calls with family today, so I figured I would bring you some Christmas dinner since you might not have cooked.”

“You’re too kind. Thank you. That’s really thoughtful. Please come in.”

As I followed him inside, I looked at where to put the heavy plate of food and other bowls.

“You look nice,” a voice echoed behind me.

“Thanks,” I responded. Now we started conversing as he asked me what I had been up to. Me and my long stories, have

I forgotten I have guests at my flat. Poor Tee, she is going to booshume me for leaving her with Dani and her fiancé, whom she hardly knows.

Booshume is one of those words I have made up since I was much younger. It can be for many meanings but none pleasant, of course. I quickly told him I had guests and this was a short visit and went through what I had brought for him to eat. Then he also remembered he was still on the phone with his family.

"My family is going to ask me what took me so long and I will be telling them about being surprised with Christmas dinner. I will definitely be showing them the food and telling them who brought it for me," he said with a smirk.

"Well," I said cheekily, "maybe I should show myself to them so they can put the face to the name."

"Yeah, why not," he responded quickly. "Maybe you should," he said with a cheeky smile.

Do you want to get me in trouble by them thinking of me as a crazy woman disturbing you, I said in my head. I definitely think that's my cue to leave. I chuckled as I said my goodbye and emphasised that my guests were probably wondering what had happened to me. And within moments, I was once again in the elevator, but this time, shooting my way down while reflecting on all that had happened.

The following day, a group of us gathered for games night and potluck at Rhy's place as part of the late Christmas celebration. Good memories from the first one that made my path cross with eye candy. During games night, eye candy and I found ourselves near each other most times.

As we ate and watched the comedian, whose name I don't slightly remember, we sat next to each other. The comedian said an inappropriate joke, and I asked those in the same room with us what he meant by the joke, only for eye candy to respond. I don't need to know as it will be too much for my innocent ears. Thanks, I think.

The night was slipping away and we started playing an X-rated game. I ended up being next to him. He teased me frequently, and I responded with a touch, shove or push on him. Well, I don't know if he enjoyed it as he kept on teasing me, knowing he would get the same reaction.

At one point, we both admired Rhy's big new TV, and he wanted to take a picture of it, so, with me being me, I went and posed with the TV while he was taking the picture. Yup, only heaven knows my life right now. This flirtatiousness is too much even for my own ears and eyes.

He once again said thanks for the Christmas dinner and being too kind. Honestly, I should frame that word for him, or better, just rename his name from eye candy to 'you're too kind'.

I think he is either lost for words or limited with them, but either way…he is definitely peculiar in his own unique way, and I suppose that could be the reason why I'm not giving up yet, or it might be that I'm crazy. Hopefully, the reason is not the latter.

Chapter 5
Hints Gone Amid

Weeks went past and it's like the circle had gone back to the beginning for eye candy and me. Why does it seem like when we have made progress of a step forward, it turns again to several steps backwards?

Why do we keep on coming back to the same mountain? This is exhausting. I'm not going to bother myself. When I see him around school, I'm just going to ignore him.

Countdown till winter break has begun. One month off of relaxation and hoping to see a bit of the city.

This week at work is the final week and the students are not in school all week till Friday, the last day. Another amazing thing about this week is my big 3 0 on Thursday. Where have the years flown by?

I can promise you, I had big holiday plans for turning into this new decade. But with all that is happening in our world, I'm just grateful to be alive and in good health. Hopefully, next year, I will re-celebrate this beautiful milestone.

Last Tuesday, Dani and I decided to bake a banana cake after work. My baking buddy of delicious treats. It's been a while since I made it, and with the tons of ripe bananas, we ended up baking three banana cakes.

Once again, I found myself making my way to eye candy's building with some cake for him. I know right, I don't learn, do I? But you know what, I love food and love making people happy with it. I arrived once again at his door. This time, as he mentioned how kind I was, I responded with whatever.

Surely if you believe it, you would stop having two personalities with me and taking us around the mountain of nowhere. But this time, as I left his place, I took back my things from the Christmas dinner I brought him previously and then the plate from today as he placed it in his own dishes. With a goodbye, this was the final time in my heart I'd decided to bring him food.

I mean, by now, if he hasn't figured out I like him and would want us to be friends, there is no hope for him. If he hasn't guessed that's my intention, then the only other option is I want to overfeed him and make him lose his figure with food or rather kill him with overfeeding. What a laugh.

Guys are indeed slow. They are indeed different creatures from women, and I won't deny their existence on another planet.

Back again to this special week. Today is Wednesday, and we've training we had to attend most of the day. I'm not looking forward to it. Especially as I've been feeling discomfort with heartburn. Yesterday, I asked several people if they had heartburn tablets, and no one had. I also thought I had brought some with me from the U.K., but I hadn't packed any.

Usually, I'm good with things like that, especially as heartburn usually recurs to me every so often for as long as I can remember. I mean, I even swallow my spit by messaging eye candy asking for any heartburn tablets due to being in severe pain.

'Random question, but do you by any chance have anything for heartburn?' I sent it out to him.

'Good question. I haven't broken hearts in a while. Ha-ha. But no, I don't have anything. I don't have any medicine at all actually', he responded.

Well, I do say this guy has jokes. I came out of the shower to see his messages. I didn't know whether to insult him for my pain or cry out with laughter at his terrible joke. One thing I do give him credit for is he does have a way to make me laugh with his quirky sense of humour.

'Ha-ha, are you sure, you haven't? Oh dear…do you have normal milk instead? At least I could take my dairy tablet after since milk usually helps with heartburn', I say back in reply to his message.

'You're right', he responded to the heartbreak question. 'I have almond milk instead'.

Good gracious, I have almond milk too, I say to myself. But let me be nice by saying to him I don't know if almond milk will work. So I did, and after that message, that was it. I didn't hear from him again.

Once again, he hasn't failed to prove me wrong. He has withdrawn again. Anyway, I'm off to bed as the training is tomorrow and I don't feel too great.

As I walked into the computer lab for training, I struggled to find a spare seat. This is what happens when you don't arrive first. Hopefully, this training will be good as I've part two of it soon after this one. As the training was about to start, hold and behold who enters the same training room…yes, eye candy.

Why me? Why did he have to choose the same training when there were about seven other options to choose from? I really couldn't be bothered to see him in the same place today. Anyway, who cares? He then makes his way to the front seats. At least I was at the back, and we weren't near each other.

The training continued and it was long-winded. Throughout, I kept thinking to myself, *why oh why did I choose here?* They advertised it so well but I should have known it was too good to be true. It's always the same with an advertisement on the TV.

They usually sell you false hopes and lies. During the training, I had to swap places from where I was sitting comfortably with another teacher as she needed the plug near me for her laptop.

Guess where I ended up sitting? Let's just say not too far off from eye candy. Finally, the training was finished but I still needed to endure another session with the same virtual trainer. It seemed like I'm the only one that double took the two-part to this training. As my colleagues left me, I turned and realised I wasn't the only one from the first training who chose the second part of the training. Eye candy also chose it.

As we all waited for the next session to begin and other staff to join us, eye candy turned and said to me, "Is your heartburn better?"

Well, I say, I'm shocked you still remember even though it was only yesterday evening we converse messages. "Well," being cheeky, I responded it was a bit better, and decided to point out why he went so quiet after my last message and didn't respond. He was gobsmacked and replied it's not totally accurate.

I even went further by saying to a friend who was next to us if I was ever in danger, I know who not to message because he tends not to respond to my messages, and that friend shouldn't also contact him in emergency cases. My goodness, only heaven knows where the boldness is coming from. All I know is I left eye candy speechless.

Before the training started, we all had to sign in again, even those who were here previously. So eye candy asked me to sign for him on the paper. Sure, no worries, I responded as I signed myself in. As the training was starting, my team lead and eye candy team leader, who were both next to me on either side, kept on wanting to talk to each other.

So at the end, where did I end up moving, the next available seat next to eye candy. Yup, I'm also surprised how this happened, but oh well. The training went on, and in between, eye candy and I kept on interacting and conversing conversation.

Then something dawned on me; I realised I had signed the wrong person and not eye candy's name with my lack of focus earlier. Oh no. Why me. Now I have to remember to rectify it before I shoot off to my next training after.

Well, the training finished and I began to rush my way down the four flights of stairs. Then I realised I hadn't rectified the signing-in mistake. So I quickly shoot over to eye candy classroom to tell him, only to find him with his team lead having a conversation. Badly interrupting them as my next training awaited me, I told him the mistake I did.

Only for him to then say, he realised I didn't sign him in properly and has already done so. This guy, hey, he made me anxious and worry for no reason. I walked away, leaving him and his team leader having no words but shaking off the head for him.

The big 30 day is already today. No way. This week has been too quick. As birthday wishes swamped my phone, especially from school chats, hold and behold whose message came through privately…eye candy, saying happy birthday and hope I celebrate it well this weekend.

With me being cheeky, I responded, thanks, and where is he taking me to celebrate it well. Only for him to say, I'm right, and he hadn't thought of that…so the cheek continued from my end since it's my birthday after all. I responded that he had until the end of today to find somewhere to go.

I know, right? Either I'm courageous and taking the bull by the horn, or I was crazy to send such a message. Then silent as a ghost, I didn't hear back from him. Anyway, it's my birthday, so who cares. No sadness on this day but rather celebrating life, and any tears that will be released from my eyes, will be tears of joy.

Chapter 6
The Plan and Kidnap Plot

Wow, I can't believe it's already been almost a week—the first sweet week of the winter break. Relaxation was not a joke indeed. That's precisely what I have been doing. Also, I did a birthday staycation on the first night of the holiday.

I've also completed the school work I had brought home and had my Chinese lesson. So far, not been a bad first week, especially as the Christmas tree has been taken down. I must say, I never understood how the tree could be packaged in the box nicely when you first buy it, and after you've finished lavishing it on display in your home and try to re-package it, it becomes a mission impossible.

No matter how much you try to package it in box, you end up struggling in defeat. However hard you try, it just won't get back inside the same box properly. I mean, come on, the package is your home till the December month strike back. Just accept your fate, tree.

I have salsa class later and I will try to pre-relax till then. Mmm, I wonder how eye candy is getting on so far with the first week of winter break almost finished. Well, I'm not going to ponder on it, but I will reach out with a message; be the bigger person, if I may say so myself.

Honestly, I don't know why I'm bothering to be his friend. But that question didn't stop me from reaching out. So here I go.

'Are you having a good week so far?' I sent the message.

'Honestly, it's alright. I haven't been doing much, if I'm honest. What's your week been like?', he responded not long after.

'But have you had time to rest and unwind. It's been very relaxing...basically the same as yours', I then say.

'Well, I've had a few days where I've stayed in and watched TV shows, so I'd say so, ha-ha', he says.

'Hehe, that's definitely resting and unwinding...if only I knew, I would've come and disturbed you', I cheekily replied.

'Ha-ha, you should have; I welcome it', he wrote back.

'[Chuckle] I will keep that in mind for this week. Are you all prep for your upcoming trip...or should I say the trip you're gate-crashing your couple friend', I messaged back.

'Well, it looks like I'm cancelling it, as the quarantine rules are a bit of a pain. I will end up staying in Shanghai the whole time, I reckon. Maybe do a staycation just for the fresh bed sheets and morning buffet breakfast', he then said.

'Oh dear, that's a shame but wise idea, though. That sounds like a plan...I recommend the one I went to last week; it was divine. Let's just say I didn't want to leave after', I wrote back.

'Which one did you go to? Just one night?', he responds.

'Blackstone M+. Yeah, it was just one night...when are you planning on going?', I responded.

'No idea. I'll have a look tonight', he says.

‘Cool stuff…if not, I’m sure there are other options too; it all depends what type of hotels you’re into’, I wrote back.

‘Any plans for the rest of the break?’, he said.

‘Nothing over the top, so far just KTV, art class, craft night & games. What about you, apart from staycation, what are your other plans?’, I messaged back.

‘Good question. Trying to furnish my apartment properly and then be a Shanghai tourist pretty much’, he messaged back.

‘You’re trying to furnish your apartment without a hint of me in the decision?’, I cheekily wrote.

‘You’re right; how could I have forgotten!’, he says.

‘Ha-ha will let you off since I’m nice, as long as there is a hint of green since it’s my favourite colour. As a tourist, I think you may need a tour guide, aka me’, I said.

‘Well, if that’s the case, I’m looking for a speakeasy bar downtown’, he wrote back.

‘Mmm, good choice…As a tour guide, when will your tour be there?’, I responded.

Then as quiet as a mouse, the conversation stopped. For nearly three days, our messages seemed endless and effortless. Almost believing we had handled the big mountain that we previously circled around. But hey, once again, only heaven knows.

Today is Monday, already. A new week and I’m off to IKEA with Kraft. I am looking forward to it. Getting more homely things for my apartment gets me excited. Besides, who doesn’t love IKEA shopping visits? Especially now my Christmas tree is gone, I need something nice to replace that area.

And who is the perfect handyman to fix whatever I buy? Well, who else except eye candy. Also, I thought of it last night. I could turn up at his door with ingredients for us to cook together, and afterwards, I would ask him to come over to mine and fix whatever piece of furniture I had bought.

What a perfect kidnap plot, if I may say so myself. Soon the FBI or CSI will be recruiting me. As long as the mission is not abolished, or even worse, he ruins it by not being in his house. It's been a day since he has disappeared from his response to my last message, but that doesn't bother me.

I think he is just against his phone, or even worse, he has forgotten how to write. Anyway, for the sake of my new furniture and home, the kidnap plot must proceed.

During the IKEA visit, I started pondering over my thoughts. What if it's not a wise idea? Great, now I'm doubting myself. What could plan B be? What if I invite him over first to fix the furniture and then head off to his place to chill and cook.

Besides, I seasoned the chicken last night, and I have my groceries delivered before 2 pm. *That sounds perfect*, as I thought about the whole thing. As soon as IKEA shopping finished, I said goodbye to Kraft and sat in the Didi taxi. Mmm, should I send a message now or wait till I get home. It's now 12-ish.

What if he has plans for today? The thought came oozing through my mind. Oh great, now I'm overthinking. Oh well, I reassured myself. I'm just going to send a generic message and see if he is busy. Based on his response, I will know if I should go ahead with the impossible mission.

I sent a message asking if he was busy. No turning back now as the Didi taxi smoothly drive me home. 'Just making lunch. What's up?', the response came back from him.

With a deep sigh of disappointment at his lunch, I doubted if my plan would even work now. Yet again, I responded that I needed his help teaching me how to fix something unless I would never learn. He was like, he will be over in 20 minutes. But knowing that would not give me plenty of time to get home and feeling bad that he was in the middle of his lunch, I told him not to rush but to come over in an hour.

As I arrived home, my music went on, and I started unpacking my IKEA shopping, still debating on the kidnap of the cooking since he had just eaten. Not long after, a knock came on my door. Cheerfully, I opened the door with a warm greeting. "Would you like slippers for your feet? But they are pink," I asked him.

"Yes," he responded, "I don't mind."

"Don't worry, you're in luck," I then say. "I have this new hotel one and I think they will fit your feet too."

"Thank you," he replied.

We got lost in conversations before he could even begin fixing the coffee table. He sat on the chair as I sat on the sofa and we started catching up. Then one conversation led to the next, and in no time, I was telling him about my salsa journey experience the other day, in which I got lost getting to the city on a train and then my journey to Shanghai and how I ended up in first class.

Blown away by how in detail I could tell a story; he was literally lost for words, my words.

"I'm off to the garden centre to get some plants on Wednesday or Thursday. You can join me if you want," he then said out of the blue and not even in the line of what we were speaking about.

"Sure," I responded, blown away that he could even be so friendly, and asked.

"Just let me know the time you wish to go," I then said.

As he opened the box to start fixing the coffee table, I told him I was leaving him for a bit to pick up my groceries which had just arrived at the gate. "Do you need help with it?" He then said.

"No, there are not many things I got," I responded. I did not know what awaited me downstairs. I arrived downstairs to realise that I had purchased a lot of things with two big bottles of water. Oh man, why didn't I accept the help he offered? Now I have to suffer carrying these things.

I huffed and puffed as I made my way back to my flat from the entrance gate. Arriving back at the flat, I was glad someone had made themselves very comfortable. As I began to unpack, I asked if he would like a drink. "Yeah, just water, thanks."

If he only knew it was a rhetorical question. I have already prepared the sparkling apple cider bottle. I responded with, "Nah, I already got a drink for us." I handed him the bottle to open and took down two wine glasses. As he opened for us, he asked me why I don't drink and what a perfect way to tell another detailed story. So I began telling the story as I poured the drinks and handed him his glass.

During the story, I carried on unpacking and revealed to him the confession of my kidnap cooking plan. He responded that if only he had known of it beforehand, because now he had just eaten. But being cheeky once again, I asked if he was busy tonight, and he said he had a phone call to a family member that takes place every Monday at 7-ish.

So being bossy once again, I said that's plenty of time since it was just around 2-ish. We could still chill and cook together. With the idea of not having everything at his home we might need, we decided to stay in my flat and chill and cook instead.

With three options given to him, he responded with, he doesn't mind. Typical guy, hey. So I ended up mainly choosing the meal to cook, but he did decide on the type of potatoes we should have.

As he finished fixing the coffee glass table, he came and joined me in the kitchen, and we cooked together while flowing with endless conversations once again. I began to hear what he was saying and spoke less so I could also know more about him. I started seeing him as a friend. I was learning more about him, and it felt just right.

A moment I would have liked to treasure and replay at a later stage. I also realised he was becoming more comfortable around me and letting his guard down. His warm smile, laughter, and quirky sense of humour were all part of his makeup. Making himself more comfortable, he started opening my cupboards to see what I had and looked at each picture on my wall to build a story of who I really was.

His guards continued to be let down as he began to share a bit about his family and his experience of things he had gone through that shaped his life so far. Moreover, he shared how he ended up being in Shanghai during such a time. Time indeed became endless, and I secretly wished moments of this will recur over and over again so I could get to know him more.

As the food was nearly ready, he began to mix the batter mixture for the pancakes and prepare the strawberries and blueberries we would have alongside it. "What happened to the mixture?" I asked.

"Does the quantity looks correct? I think you may need to help me out," he responds.

So without hesitation, I praised and admired his effort as it was his first time making the mixture and helped him to fix it. Then he reminded me of the day I brought him the pancakes and how much he enjoyed it as he loves pancakes. Who would have guessed, hey? I had even forgotten about that first moment.

As I dished our dinner, he kept on complimenting how nice the chicken sauce smelled. In my heart, I was secretly praying it also tasted as good as it smelled. Don't get me wrong, I can cook, but this afternoon, half of my mind was distracted by him. So only heaven knows what spices I was using. Just praying in my heart that he actually loves the taste.

As I handed him the plate, I asked if I should move the centrepiece from the table since my table is relatively small and the centrepiece took most of the space. "No," he responded. "It looks too nice."

So we both sat opposite each other with our plate of food ready to be consumed. After pouring some more apple cider into our wine glasses, he initiated us to toast with the glasses and we began to eat and kept talking away. He told me he would clean and wash up as we finished dinner.

I was surprised as earlier he had already confessed that he doesn't like cleaning and washing up, and I admitted that I usually like a clean kitchen to know I've done an excellent job. As he began cleaning and washing up, I made a start on frying the pancakes.

"What oil would you prefer us to use, olive or sunflower?" I asked him.

"I don't mind, whichever one you think is best," he replied.

Mmm, I did the first one with olive oil, trying to experiment and make it healthy for him, but I rather stick to sunflower oil, which I know and usually use.

After the pancakes were finished frying, we sat down again for dessert. We had fruits to choose from and different spreads like honey and chocolate spread for the pancakes. As the last pancake piece was eaten from his plate, he cheekily opened his mouth and said, "Would you like me to give you the overall rating now?"

"Sure," I responded. "Go for it," I cheekily responded.

"Well," he said. "Overall, I will give everything 8/9."

"Oh really now," I said. I have no words for this guy's sense of humour right now.

"Yes, it was really good, especially the chicken. But everyone always needs a way forward in everything. That's why I didn't give you a 10," he cheekily replied while laughing.

"Very funny," I said, laughing back. "No worries, I hear you loud and clear."

I packed some food for him to take home as he finished washing up, even though he said I didn't have to. "Nah, we both made this food, so we will both finish it off," I told him. And besides, does he want me to be the only one gaining the calories. I don't think so.

Finishing off the last bit of plate to wash up, we both sat back down on the chair and lifted my mini Uno game; I looked at him and echoed out, "If you have time for a game?"

"Sure. But I'm not going to be a gentleman in this as I like to win," he replied.

"Well, well, well, today you've met your match as I like to win too," I blurted back out. "Growing up during Christmas time, games will always be played with my family; let's just say, they dreaded playing games with me. By the way, do you know how to play?" I said back with a smirk.

"Of course I do," he shrieked with a chuckle.

"Okay, let the game begin and prepare to lose," I proudly said back to him.

The game heated up between us as I introduced the rule card. "I give you the rule to pick up five extra cards," I told him.

"What? Surely you just made up that rule?" he said back in disbelief of what I had just done.

"Nope, it's my rule for the blank card. You can make up any rules. I thought you said you've played this version," I say.

"I'm so going to search the rules when I get home and teach you because you're cheating," he replied.

"Ha, don't be a sore loser because I'm winning," I confidently replied.

The game continued to heat up as he gave me rules of picking up as well. When we thought we were almost done with the game, we found ourselves back to stage one. Eventually, we were both left with two cards each. I placed one of my cards down while echoing Uno and whispered a prayer in my heart that I had made the right choice and hoped to win.

He placed one of his cards and also echoed Uno. Then suddenly, I stood up and did a victory dance as I was about to put my final card down and win. His face was priceless. A guy that doesn't like losing. Well, today you've met your match as I'm a woman that doesn't like losing too.

I couldn't help but carry on my victory dancing. He said he would search the rules when he got back home and I should too because I made up extra ones. *Stop being a sore loser and better luck next time,* I thought to myself.

As he prepared to leave for his family phone call, I handed him his food to take with him. I stood by the door, ready to wave goodbye to him and thank him for fixing my table. Then out of nowhere, he stretched out his arms and hugged me tightly while thanking me for the day.

As he walked out of the door, he cheekily asked if he was now the handy tools guy who fixed my things and was only invited over when I needed something fixing. And without hesitation, I cheekily replied he doesn't just have to come round when I asked him to fix things, but he was always invited to come and chill with me. He said okay with a gentle smile as he made his way to the lift.

I closed the door in amazement at precisely what happened with my day. Was it all a dream? Am I about to just wake up and laugh at myself? Was everything that happened today real? It's nearly 7 pm, and I've spent most of my day with eye candy.

What a day well spent, and now I'm sure things can only go uphill from here with our friendship. The mountain is now a tiny puddle we stepped over, and what a big relief.

Chapter 7
The Shocking Truth: How Did I Miss That?

Wednesday morning came, and I woke up. Sometimes I really believe my body is an alarm clock of its own. Later on in the day, I'm spending time with Joony. Now I still hadn't heard from eye candy since Monday evening when he left my apartment, but I give him the benefit of the doubt on his ghosting.

Still, I wonder if the gardening centre is still happening today. And if so, what time will it happen? I definitely don't want to miss my day with Joony or even be late to meet her. To stop my mind from wandering again, I messaged him and asked what time the garden centre visit would be.

Silent as a feather, I only heard back from him an hour later. I know it was still early morning, but I'm an early riser, and I've already started getting ready, so why isn't he up the time I was up. Now let's open his message and see what time we are going; even though confirmations were not previously made, I can only assume everything was still on for today.

'Ah, change of plans, will probably go next week instead', he wrote.

Is he for real? Would he have messaged me if I hadn't reached out? Right, eye candy, you need to be booshume. That is plain rude. Anyway, I will carry on getting ready since I have plans with Joony. I responded to him after I had calmed myself down.

As quiet as a ghost once again he became after I responded. I honestly wish I could read through what goes on in his head. But for now, I've got a beautiful afternoon that I will be spending with Joony, and I don't want to ruin it with thoughts about him.

Joony and I began to catch up during our mani and pedi session. Hold and behold, I blurted out everything to her about eye candy as the situation still bothered me. Why, oh, why does it bother me so much? I know something is up with him, but I can't quite put my finger on what it is. I wish he would just be honest with me.

After the long catch-up with Joony and her updating me on what has been happening with her, we worked ourselves an appetite. In no time, we were dining at 'Elements Fresh'. During our dinner, eye candy's conversation came up again, and Joony asked if I was friends with him on Instagram.

"Nope, it had not even crossed my mind. Right now, I'm just annoyed with his attitude, and I know something is up. I only wished for him to be honest and tell me," I responded with a sigh.

"Well," Joony replied. "Why don't you ask him, and be honest with him by telling him that you like him and you don't appreciate the way he is treating you…"

Well, now she spoke it out loud, it does make sense. Why didn't I think of this before but instead, I've allowed my mind to be clouded. One thing led to another, and the next thing

Joony did, left me baffled. She decided to go on eye candy's Instagram page to investigate. Well, my curiosity also got the best of me, and I began to look through on her phone.

Oh no, what my eyes saw next, they were not prepared for it. Nooo, I mean, I had a feeling, but I was trying to deny it. "Joony, I think this is his girlfriend." The words came rushing out of my mouth with no warning. How did I miss that? Oh gracious me, I feel so silly. That makes sense now on why he has been hot one minute and cold with me the next.

"Well, this is not healthy. I'm coming off his page." I handed Joony back her phone and caught my breath again. There is only one thing to do now. I'm going to message him once I return home and ask him so he can confirm. Social media is not going to reveal this truth to me. Instead, it should come from the horse's mouth.

But did he even owe me anything to have to tell me in the first place? And do I have any right to demand the truth from him?

By the time I arrived home, time had gone way past. It was nearly 10-ish, and only heaven knows if he was still awake. Still, I'm taking away this constant thought from my mind and sending him a message. Now how do I put it without being too forward? After all, it's not my business if he does have a girlfriend. Is it?

Well, who cares, whose business it is? I'm just going to ask. The worst thing he can do is confirm my investigation is accurate. So here we go. I sent the message without thinking twice or even saying hi; just typed it like this… 'Random question…do you have a girlfriend?'

With the message sent, there was nothing else I could do but sleep and wait for his response in the morning. Hopefully, my message is not the first message he wakes up to in the morning. Now, it's time for my beauty sleep and brain rest.

Dawn was now breaking, and I was up again, rise and shine. I got on with my day by doing bits and pieces before the KTV with some friends later. Then a message came through from him. The moment of truth has finally arrived.

'Morning. Yes, I do'.

Chapter 8
Is This Goodbye?

Well, I say. If I was not lost for words before, I believe now I am. How do I even respond to that message? I wish he had only told me sooner, then he wouldn't have had to be in guilt mode all this time. That's if he was ever in guilt mode. Anyways, I have to reply him…mmm what do I say not to make things even more awkward than it is.

'Morning, that makes sense…is that the reason why you've been refusing my friendship', I wrote with a smirk to try and ease the awkwardness if that was even possible.

'Hahaha, what you on about? Who says I'm refusing your friendship', he responds.

'Your actions say, hahaha. I understand because I know you're an observant wise guy. I know you've already guessed I am interested in you, especially as it's not any guy I cook with or for. But it makes sense why your guards are extremely high because women can be very dangerous.

'Still, I would like to be your friend as long as you don't fall for me due to your stomach, and I promise not to cross the line. Right…now I feel like we can start on a blank new page since the elephant in the room has been dealt with', I replied with a laugh to myself at how shocked I was by taking the bull by the horn.

Wow, did I really just send that long message to him. Am I okay? *No temperature*, I thought to myself as I placed my hand on my head. Well, only heaven knows why I sent him all that. All I know is that my chest feels lighter than before. Now, it feels like I'm floating on cloud nine.

Not long after, a message came through from him. 'Haha, there's no elephant in the room. I like hanging out with you. Well, they do say good food is the way into a man's heart'.

I have to say, after receiving the last message, I don't know if I actually felt at ease. Would I be comfortable with all this if I was in his girlfriend's position and in another country? Frankly speaking, the answer is NO. I know me; I'm a jealous person of things that matter to me and things that are my own. So my conviction was beginning to kick in once again.

The evening came, and I was off to karaoke but still had not responded to his message from this morning. I was still unhappy with the whole situation and I knew I needed to send a message back to him, but a wise one. But I can't collect my thoughts right now to do so.

After a couple of hours of karaoke fun, I arrived back home around 10-ish. I needed a voice of reasoning, and my cousin is good at that. After an hour of pouring my heart into her, I finally got the answer I was looking for. Here we go again, another long message I'm now going to send him, which he will be waking up to.

'Hiya…just came from KTV and getting a chance to respond to you. Just reflected on your last message. Yes, the saying is right that the way to a man's heart is by good food.

I also agree to like hanging out with you, but I don't trust myself with you because I have feelings for you and for our safety, I think it is best I don't disturb you and let you be', I send it to him without reading it twice.

There is certainly no turning back from that message and I honestly don't know how he would take it. Even though I don't know how I would take it in his position, it is what it is. I don't want to feel guilty even if I thought something was there and desired his friendship.

I would rather be at peace and guilt-free when sleeping at night. Not long after, I dozed off into the night after reassuring myself everything will work out the way it needed to in the end.

Morning came, and I carried on with my bright and early day again. Not long after, a message came from him.

'Alright, Sarah, sounds good'.

As I read his message, I withheld any inch of tears that wanted to play a trick on my eyes. I suppose this was goodbye.

I couldn't believe the ending crept up out of nowhere while the beginning was still being written.

Only time will tell why things had to happen the way they did rather sooner than later. Still, I was glad to get out of this sooner than later. Learning from my mistake of the past, a couple of years ago.

Let's just say, if I knew what I know now and had the courage and boldness that I have now, I would have absolutely made wiser choices than be involved in something that was never meant to be mine. But now, the same kind of thing has been presented to me, and thank God for the strength to walk away before bridges are broken and burned, once again, with me on it.

Only heaven knows what will happen when I see him around work. But one thing I do know is I won't stop being me and authentic to myself. I will keep to my word of staying away, but I won't be spiteful by not saying hi to him when our paths cross.

I will always treasure the moments when I believed we were friends because each conversation and moment shared were real, and seeds were being planted in my open heart for more remarkable blossoming growth.

Chapter 9
From Eye Candy to Nicorn-Poo...

When you think you know someone, that's when you are far off from knowing them. The saying is so true that not all which glitter glows. Things are never what they seem if we only uncover and dig to find the absolute truth.

It's been two weeks now since the big reveal and no conversation has tunnelled between myself and eye candy. As each passing day goes by, my heart becomes more accepting. Equally, for my mind, let's just say each day is a new day. Time will surely pass by, and this will soon be distant even to reach.

Not long after coming back from Korean BBQ with some of the ladies, I received a message from Joony (oh Korean BBQ, how I love thee). Honestly, the day the soles of my feet touched down South Korea, I don't know how I will contain the joy in me, apart from spending each passing day eating one Korean BBQ after the next.

God help my weight after that visit. I would have to be on a soup diet for a month. Still, I love South Korea so much and it's almost like love at first sight. More like the sight from what I've been sold on the K dramas and movies. Good old K dramas and movies, only they can rock it so well.

Heaven knows if another race even attempts such films, they will just stick out like sore thumbs. For their sake of sanity, they should dare not try to copycat the Koreans.

'Baby girl, let me call you around 3', the message came through from Joony.

Mmm, I genuinely wonder what it could be about. I mean, less than an hour ago, I was just with her at the Korean BBQ. I wonder what happened. Maybe she's not able to make it to our girly night tomorrow.

Okay Sarah, chillax. Just relax your mind as you wait for the call. Easier said than done, especially when watching a teen movie with my director hat on of what could be even better in this movie.

In no time, my phone began to ring. "Hello, darling," I answered. As the conversation continued, she brought to my mind the reason why she wanted to call so urgently.

"Well, my dear, I don't know whom you have shared the story concerning you and eye candy but let's just say Ta-Ta was running her mouth like water to me earlier about it and..."

What, how is this possible. I say to myself. Are we back in high school? Do people have anything better to do with their life instead of gossiping about others? As Joony spoke, a thousand and one thoughts skipped in my head and all the possible outcomes to respond to this piece of information.

As I gathered my thoughts and hung up the phone, a weight of heavy clouds fell on my shoulders. What? How is this possible? It's normal to like a guy and want to be their friend. But why was I like this? Why the agitation and annoyance over what I've heard.

Am I annoyed because people are gossiping about me? I mean, of course. Who can testify and say I want to be talked about? Only those who decide to deceive themselves. Honestly, the truth of the matter was, I don't want eye candy to hear I've been spreading his name on what happened with us. He may think I'm a loose-mouth woman, and I'm far off from it.

Should in case he wanted to be my friend, he won't be able to trust someone like me if he thinks this is my personality. Still, I'm not too bothered about what he will think, to be honest. The truth of the matter is, I'm not like that and I don't want to be perceived like that.

I only briefly shared with Kraft what had happened with eye candy and how we were no longer friends. Kraft, who is my friend, is also close with Ta-Ta. But I trust Kraft and I know she won't go and share my business with others, especially as she has no right.

Still, if Ta-Ta knows and she is gossiping about me, it could have only been Kraft who shared with her. I mean, it must be, isn't it? Right, this frustration is too much for my heart. I can't take it anymore. I want to deal with this issue. I need to find out the truth.

I can't and won't allow myself to overthink and be drained out because of this matter. I've come too far to be able to voice and talk things out now. No longer the person who would just keep quiet and allow things to eat me up inside like a worm inside an apple.

Okay, I'm calling Kraft. Ring…ring…ring; still no answer. It's okay. I will just send her a message saying I would like to talk to her.

As I attempted to return to the movie I was watching to distract me, I was far from focused. In fact, now I was coming up with plans beyond what words to say and how to nip this situation in the bud before it spreads like wildfire.

Mmm, maybe I could message eye candy and give him a heads up on what has happened and justify that it's inaccurate what the rumours are saying, and I'm not a loose mouthed woman. Hold on. *Wait, Sarah. Now you're acting crazy. Stop this overreaction.*

I give you permission to stop overthinking and wait. Calm down. Leave your house and go for a walk to pick up your deliveries to ease your mind from this situation as it's not healthy at all. Okay, that's exactly what I will do.

As I strolled along the neighbourhood with one of my friends, a message came through from Krafts. While me and her converse in messages, the truth is finally unfolded. Oh God, how stupid do I look now? The last two hours of overthinking were a waste of my brain space. *Brain, please hear me when I say I'm sorry.*

My emotions ran faster than lightning and a tornado. Now I've lost respect for this nicorn-poo. Yes, the name has changed. He doesn't deserve to be eye candy any longer. How could he? Is he crazy? All this time, I was wrong.

I mean, not many times I could say that about guys I like, but hey, it goes to show no one is perfect. Definitely, not all that glitter is gold. The rust can be creeping depending on where it has been positioned. And may I say, the saying is valid for this nicorn-poo.

I sincerely have no words. In fact, I don't want to waste my words on him. But can you believe what this guy had been up to? This guy has been seen coming out of another woman's house in early hours of the morning by more than one person. Yes, I know what you're thinking. I'm just exaggerating again, but no, not this time.

This time I have every right to overreact. Also, he has been leading on this other woman that works in his team and he is now acting like a smug to her. Things are indeed beginning to make sense. What did Joony say before when we had gone out for the mani and pedi day, and we were eating dinner? She said that she had seen him on the tinder app during the December period. Why didn't I hear it?

Oh God, me and my self-selective hearing. Why are some men like this? I know I can't speak for the whole men race as he doesn't represent them all, but I am speechless with his behaviour. Yes, I know he is only a human being, but hell no. What about his GIRLFRIEND? The number one person I considered when I decided to shut the door that was open with him.

I'm a woman, and moreover, I have a conscience. I want to sleep peacefully at night without guilt eating up my peace of mind. What the heck is he playing at? Is he for real? If I were to ask him questions right now, they would be endless.

Are you not in a relationship? Did you not utter that you were in one to me? So why on earth are you playing around? Are you lonely? Is it desperation that you want to fill a temporary void? Whatever it is; frankly it's definitely not my business.

Fortunately, I have had a lucky escape. I certainly do not want to be caught up with someone like that, especially as he is not the best thing since sliced bread. I remembered being sent a quote that states, 'Never lie to a woman because she's going to find out anyway. Most women investigate better than FBI'. I can testify to this being true.

Reflecting on how he had devoured my anointed chicken a couple of weeks back, damaging it to the core, makes me want to slap him with the wind for his silly actions. That meat was made with love, and he thinks it was in vain consuming that fire cooker that kept on turning off. All I can say from this experience is, if I wasn't sure before, now I can be sure that God watches my back.

I'm truly loved because I don't want to find myself in a sticky situation with him. I'm so happy not to feel sad telling anyone about what had happened between us and not having him as a friend. I'm just glad that I can still be myself.

Whenever I see him around, I will just be my natural self, say hi with the compassion of you were so not worth it, especially having my friendship. I'm just going to carry on living life; after all, the best is yet to come for me.

Chapter 10
Vacation Wrapped Up: The Park

Where has it all gone to? Wasn't just the other day winter vacation was beginning? Why is today the last day of it? Oh well, it's a good thing some of my colleagues have planned for us to spend the day at C-Park as the weather will be really sunny and hot. Let me go and embrace Vitamin D into my cells.

Now, who said they were going again. As I was about to shower, I double-checked the names. Oh, cool, there are about 8 of us. I can't wait as it's going to be fun. Even Dat is going to be there. I mean, only 3 guys are going to be there. One of them is my friend's husband. The other is Rhy and the final one Dat.

It's been a bit of time since I saw Dat, and I wonder if he has been behaving himself and not getting caught up with many women. Let's just say I won't be holding my breath up for him because he can't help himself but flirt with any beautiful woman.

Soon after I came out of the shower, my phone blasted with messages from the group page. Oh yes, someone decided to make a group page with all of us in it, regardless it will only be used for today. That doesn't matter. That person is Rhy and Eva, who were trying to kill birds with one stone concerning communicating with others. Don't get me wrong, I don't judge them because I see sense in that.

Dee was now asking questions about things that she would bring along. After all, everyone was contributing their part. As for me, sweets and snacks. I could not be bothered even to make something fancy. As I read through the messages to catch up on if I had missed anything, hold and behold, what did my eyes saw…Nooo! What? How is this possible.

Mmmm, okay, no comment. Nicorn-poo is also part of the group. Then my eyes saw Eva's message saying, '…he is now coming too'. Well, well, well, our paths will be crossing each other sooner than I had expected.

So, I was going to wear a dress. Well, that idea has now gone out of the window. What other beautiful short summer clothes do I have because that will be what I'm wearing today. He will see and realise today what a priceless jewel he failed to recognise in front of him.

Obviously, that priceless jewel being me, 100%. Okay, shorts and a nice top, plus my red shoulder-less cardinal, should in case the weather turns against us all. Why should my skin suffer from the cold just for looking nice?

Soon, it was almost time to meet everyone at the front gate so we could decide how we would head off to the park. Can you believe all of us are a group of educators but we are also very indecisive and into last-minute decision making? Skilful, hey. Since I was early and there was still another 25 minutes until we met at the gate, I decided to go up to Dee's building and wait with her.

Arriving at Dee's place, I began to wait with her as we communicated. She couldn't take it any longer. Then she burst out loud, "Girl, I wanna ask you something but don't know how to put it."

Mmm, I think I know where this conversation is going. So interrupting her, I said, "Girl, I think I know what you are about to say. Is it how I'm feeling to know nicorn-poo is also joining us today?"

"Yes," she said with a raised voice.

"Well," I said. "I actually don't care. We were bound to cross paths anyway. After all, we have some of the same group of friends and colleagues. Also, I made sure I'm looking on point so when he sees me, he will know I'm too priceless." Dee couldn't help but laugh and said she admired my style and confidence.

We soon left her apartment to head to the gate and waited for the others.

The moment of truth had arrived. Here he comes majestically walking towards us.

"Okay, Sarah, act normal," I whispered to myself. Before he could fully reach us with Eva, I quickly opened my mouth and said, "Hiya…"

"Hiya," he replied without hesitation. And then I carried on talking to Rhy about the conversation we had previously been having. Dee then started complaining about how heavy her bags were even after Rhy and Sammy volunteered to help.

"No, it's okay," she said. "When we get to the other gate to meet the others, I will rent the bike to the station and meet you guys there since you're all going to walk."

Without a moment to spare, we started our journey first to the other gate. Once again, Dee complained about her bag and others volunteered, even nicorn-poo, but still Dee said she felt terrible and she would carry on holding it. Then without hesitation, "Well, I can't be bothered to carry mine. Here you go," I confidently said to nicorn-poo. "You can carry my bag of things."

The others were gobsmacked by what they had just witnessed. "What?" One said. "Your bag is not even heavy."

"I know," I said, smirking, "but he's not carrying anything, and I want to walk in style without a bag."

As he grabbed the bag from me, he was also in disbelief. "Am I now holding your bag?" he said to me.

"Of course," I cheekily said as I walked majestically in front of him, trying to continue my conversation with Rhy.

As we continued to walk to the metro station, I enjoyed the sun hitting against my shoulders as my cardinal kept on dropping off on one shoulder. The whole time, I continued to joke and laugh as I made conversations with others while walking slightly ahead of nicorn-poo.

We arrived at the metro station and boarded the train to C-Park in no time. As soon as we arrived at the park entrance, we were flooded by a swamp of people.

What's all the commotion, I wonder. Only to find out, we had to scan a QR code and fill in details with payment in order to enter the park. *Oh, great*, I thought, *it's too hot for this. Why do they always have to make things so complicated? Now all this information is in Chinese. Well,* I thought again.

It's a good thing nicorn-poo and Eva can both speak and read Chinese. As Eva was helping some of the other guys, I called nicorn-poo to me. "What does it say," I asked as I gave him my screen to read.

In no time, he started sorting out the information for me. "It now needs your passport number," he says.

"Oh, great. Well, I hope I have a screenshot on my phone of it," I said quietly. I quickly began to scan through my phone. "Thank goodness," I shouted out loud. So without hesitation, I told him to get his phone out and type my passport number as I couldn't copy and paste. Let's say he didn't hesitate and just did it as a pet would, following their master's instructions.

As I went back to the information page on my phone, I asked him to read me my passport number so I could type it into the section provided. After that, I handed him my phone to finish the last steps before making the entry payment fee. Poor guy, I bet he wondered what wickedness has he done to me for me to be so demanding on him this hot day.

Well, let's just say the wickedness of stupidity of what he has been up to. But hey, that's not my place to judge. Well, at least not directly anyway.

Soon, we all entered the park and found a nice grassy spot to set up our picnic stuff.

Not long after, Eva offered me one of her tangerines. Oh man, yes, I was craving this tangerine, but I actually didn't want my hands smelling of orange. So I would have to hunt to wash my hands as logic wasn't applied by any of us to bring along wipes or a lot of bottles of water to rinse and wash hands.

Oh great, another crazy demanding idea, but who cares. I shouted his name as I walked towards him. "Please peel my tangerine for me," and without a moment to lose, I handed him my tangerine and walked away from him trying to make sense of what I had just done. *What the eck, Sarah, do you want to be insulted or even booshume by him.* Yet again, there is nothing I can do now but walk confidently.

As I sat on the other blanket, swapping my shoes and taking off my cardinal jacket, I ignored the confused stares from those around us on what was going on with nicorn-poo and I. Then his voice came to me, "Here you go," as he stretched out his hand to mine. "I decided to take a bite of the tangerine as I did the labour of peeling it."

"Rightly so, only but fair," I responded, taking the remaining tangerine from his hand. Munching away on the tasty tangerine, I couldn't help but wonder what the others were pondering regarding this situation playing out in front of them. Almost felt like the movie being played for free in front of their eyes.

With only three more tangerine pieces left in my hand, I decided to do the most decent thing, if I may say so myself. I stood confidently, walked towards him, and as I shoved them into his hand, I said, "Here you go. You can finish them." And without a moment too soon, I walked off with his 'thanks' echoing in my ears.

Not long after, the other girls started playing frisbee and I quickly joined them to keep myself busy. In no time, nicorn-poo came to join us and we all played. Let's just say my skills were below beginner level. After a while of playing this, we headed back to the grassy area where we had set up for picnic area.

As everyone began to chill and unwind, I started taking photos of myself and also with Dee.

"…Can you please move? I'm trying to take a picture of myself and you're in the way," I cheekily said to him, who could be seen through my camera lens.

"I didn't know the whole park belonged to you," he said with a smirk.

"Well, you must have missed the memo," I cheekily said back.

Walking round to the other side, I started posing away as the clicks began on the camera. But at the back of my mind, I wondered if I had been too harsh on him. I hope he realised I was only kidding. I haven't joined his snubbed and rudeness gang because I'm far from that.

As the camera continued to click, I wanted to take videos and capture time even though it was physically impossible. Once again, who was lurking in my background…the one and only, nicorn-poo. This time, I just allowed him before he decided to booshume me for being too extra.

Another frisbee round took place but this time as a piggy in the middle. Hold and behold, I ended up in the middle and the struggle was beyond real. Of course, I'm talking about the struggle of shortness as the rest of them were all taller than me, so they were throwing it around like confetti.

"You don't need to keep on running to each person; you can just stay in the middle…" he shouted to me.

Thank you, nicorn-poo…since when did you become the commentator of frisbees, I thought to myself.

Our time at the park continued. Soon, we were surrounded by young children.

Two particular boys had a football that the guys wanted to play but the kids refused. But for some reason, these boys kept on coming near me.

Mmm, I thought to myself, *I wonder if they want me to play football with them.* Okay, well, let me see, I thought to myself as I got up from the blanket. I made a gesture to them to kick me the ball, and to my surprise, they did. To be honest, I would have been so embarrassed if they also rejected me like the others because now the others were watching to see what would happen.

Then one of the kids kicked the ball to me and who would have guessed that my school days of football skills were still in me. I showed them my skills and we kept passing the ball to each other for a while. The others were shocked and jealous. “How can they allow her to play with them and they said no to us guys,” one said.

“Well,” I said, “no comment,” as I carried on playing. A bit of me wondered if nicorn-poo was staring at the whole scene. In fact, I won’t be surprised if he was looking from the corner of his eyes because I also impressed myself with some of the tricks I was pulling.

After a while of doing this, I was exhausted. These kids just didn’t get tired. They were having a blast and enjoying themselves. As for me, my younger days are no longer than in the past. I was huffing and puffing; worse than the wolf chasing the pigs.

As I ditched the kids, they were saddened and wanted to keep on playing. The other guys were saying this from what they were observing. Still, I was tired. I needed a snack in my system. That energy I lost was more than what I wanted to release for the day.

In no time, a few of the ladies and I decided to experience the electric boat ride at the other side of the park. At the same time, the guys decided to start playing another round of frisbee. So that was it, I left nicorn-poo without even minding him as I went off with the ladies.

It was such a peaceful experience on the boat, and after about an hour and a half of it, we came back to join the others. As my eyes scanned across, I realised nicorn-poo was no longer around. Mmm, do I dare to ask where he has run off too? NAH. I don't care that much.

He didn't owe me anything to say goodbye and neither did I. Within an hour later, we all packed to leave the park. As we walked back out of the gates that brought us in earlier on, I gazed at the sun and soaked up on all the sweet memories that have been established upon this day. Pondering on the thoughts of *when will our paths cross again?*

Chapter 11
The Spanner and the Impossible Filter Fix

I'm tired of this water. Enough is enough. Finally, I have decided to pay for a water filter in my shower as my skin was beginning to get eczema due to the harshness of the water. To be honest, it's more like due to the polluted water. Honestly, I had always taken water for granted growing up, but I have learned to value the most little things since living abroad.

I've been procrastinating in getting this filter since arriving in this country. Trying to outsmart what others were saying, sometimes I just seemed to forget that I wanted to purchase the filter after payday. But now I'm not waiting for payday, I will just pay for it now. So what if it is pricey, I would instead continue to have beautiful smooth skin than have it ruined by this place's water.

I contacted two companies and finally decided to go with the Korean company based on Sammy's recommendation.

It was going to arrive within a couple of days. All I can do now was wait.

On one of the days at work, I had to take one of my students to the gate as he was being picked up early. As we waited for his ayi to pick him up, I started chatting away to another colleague. After a little while, my eyes wandered and scanned through as this ayi was nowhere to be seen, and it had gone past the time she said she would collect the student.

Hold and behold who was couple feet away from me...nicorn-poo. The whole time he had been there, but I had not noticed him. Frankly enough, I didn't care, even though it was the first time seeing him since the park. I carried on pretending that I hadn't spotted him, and I believe the feeling was also mutual. Finally, the ayi came for my student and I walked back into my classroom with not a word or eye contact exchanged from either of us.

On Friday, that same week, I was just about to sit down for lunch with the students when a message came through from a name I didn't expect to see. In fact, I was shocked. So shocked that I didn't open the message straight away but got up to get a drink and double-checked that my never-failing eyes were not starting to turn against me now.

As I opened the message, it read, 'Hey, Sarah. Did you have a lovely Ayi to recommend to me? My current one always cancels last minute'.

What? Nicorn-pop just sent this? So many questions flooded my mind. But the very first one was, *did I not send you this information during the winter break, or is my memory also wanted to be against me*. Okay, no comment, I told myself. Well, I will give him the benefit of the doubt, even though I had sent it and I'm sure I wasn't the only one he could have asked. I will be the bigger person and resend it.

But before I could send the contact straight away, I couldn't help but respond first: 'Heya, sure I do, but just promise not to make her love you more than she loves me. Ouch, I hope you've been treating her right'.

By now, if he doesn't get my sense of humour, then I have no words for him.

He then responded with, 'Hahaha, you're right. Probably says more about me than her'.

After his last message, I just couldn't be bothered to respond, so I didn't. And that was it for now. I became the ghost in reply. His skill is undoubtedly rubbing off on me and I had him to thank. Even though I'm sure he was teaching it for free.

A couple of days later, my filter came for the shower but I had to install it myself as this company doesn't install it for you. I know, right. If I had paid almost double the amount, I won't even have to be stressed as installation would have been free. But no time to be stressed. I was just delighted it has finally arrived.

As I got home from work, I opened the package, ready to fix it onto my shower. Even with the videos and manual instructions on installing it, I was still confused. My goodness. If only they had a website that solved all the confusing questions you had. Even the silly ones. Their motto should be: no question is ever too stupid to ask.

I think I will take the role of the founding director. More like a self-proclaimed founding director. As I look at the spanner they sent, it seems too big. *Great, what am I going to do?* I pondered. I refuse to contact nicorn-poo to come and do it. I needed to do my self-justice by doing it on my own.

Still, I would take a picture of the spanner and send a message to ask if he had a smaller one, and would also ask Rhy as I don't trust when nicorn-poo will respond. That's if he does at all. The message went by, and nothing from both of them.

An hour went by and I was still struggling to fix this filter, and by this time, I was frustrated and tired. I nearly broke down. I don't want to sound like this but this was not for me. A man should just do it for me because I have no clue. That hour of my life, I would never get back.

Then a message came through from Rhy that he had something similar, and I could go and collect it now if I wanted. So away I went to his building. When I arrived there, he asked me the matter and I told him. Rhy, being so sweet, then decided to come with me to my apartment and help fix it. Fifteen minutes later, he completed what took me more than an hour.

"Thanks, Rhy, you're the best."

Imagine if I was still waiting to hear back from nicorn-poo. Pigs will indeed fly.

The following day, on my way to work, a message finally came in from nicorn-poo.

'Hey! I have an adjustable one? Sort of ha-ha. I'll take a pic of it when I get home'.

Literally, this guy knows how to leave me speechless. He should indeed get an award for it. It is a skill he doesn't even know he has acquired (I think).

Now, do I brutally insult him and tell him someone else has done it for me who politely responded to his messages the same day. Nah, I said to myself. I don't want to burn bridges, should in case I need it to cross by. So I responded with, okay, thank you.

After work, I mostly forgot that he said he would message me to show me what he had. Most of me said it would be a miracle if he remembers. To be honest, I had no hope in him sticking to his word. Around nearly 7.30 am, a message came through from him with a picture of the two spanners he had and saying, 'I have these'.

What? Look at nicorn-poo proving me wrong when I thought he wouldn't stick to his word. So I resend the picture message and circle one of the spanners, saying, 'This one will do', and I can get it from him if he is not busy. *But wait a minute, Sarah, isn't your filter already installed by Rhy.*

What the heck was I thinking about. As I battled the questions in my head, I thought to myself, how I don't want to seem rude and I already asked. Basically, the answers didn't make sense to me. Once again, he took his time to reply. In the meantime, my teammates had sent me this document in excel to fill from Taobao online shopping site.

I struggled as everything was in Chinese, and the form was needed by tomorrow. *Oh great*, I thought. Why did I agree to leave the house this time to pick up a spanner that I don't need anymore. Okay, well, maybe he won't reply again today or might say it's too late to pop over, and he will either bring it to work with him tomorrow to give it to me or after work.

Not long after, he replied, 'Yeah, you can come through'.

And I responded, 'I will be over shortly'. I then thought maybe he could help me with this deadline form as he speaks Chinese. So I took my laptop with me and made my way over to his building, not knowing what he would say to my response. In fact, I debated if I was indeed going to ask him.

I just wasted my hand muscle by carrying this laptop if I wasn't. As I stood in the lift waiting to go up to his floor, I carried on debating in my mind. Finally, I arrived at his front door and knocked. Without a moment to spare, he came to open the door with the spanner in his hand. As I said thank you, he turned and looked at the laptop in my hand and asked, "What's the laptop for?"

Wow, if he hadn't called it out, I would have just walked away with the spanner. So I briefly told him my deadline and wouldn't mind his help. Now it was almost 8:15 pm. I don't know how it happened but I entered his house and put my laptop on his table. We were both shocked because he partly said yes.

Actually, he said, "What do I need help with?" As he followed me to the table, he left his front door a little bit open. I explained the situation to him and he said he could only help till 8.30 pm. What? Only 15 minutes. I mean, I suppose I should be grateful as it was unannounced and he could have just said no straight away.

Before he could sit down, I told him I needed to connect to the internet. His internet was stronger and based in his bedroom like all the apartments here. So only heaven knows how clean his room was but he surely wasn't inviting me in.

He first walked into his bedroom and then said, "Actually, I will just hot spot you so you can connect to my phone internet." I think the reality of me being in his bedroom became a daunting expectation he wasn't ready to step into. Well, I didn't argue. Beggars are not choosers; I always say a beggar that chooses is not an actual beggar.

As he sat down and I stood up next to him, I told him my feet were hurting and asked how could he be happy to sit while I stood. To be honest, I pushed him away from his seat so he stood, and I sat even though he was the one helping me.

Poor guy, hey. As we searched for some of the items, he then confessed he didn't know what the Chinese character symbol meant. "What?" I shouted to him. "I thought you are fluent in both reading and writing Chinese."

"No," he responded, "my Chinese reading is not that good."

"Well," I say, "all this time, I assumed wrong." At the corner of my eye, I saw the time was almost 8:30 pm, and I felt terrible. So I told him I would leave now as it was late and it was a school night. I think he was delighted inside that I was so considerate.

As he walked me out of the door, he remarked, "Good luck with finishing this tonight because I will be sleeping."

My sense of humour kicked in again. "I hope you don't sleep till I finish this deadline. I mean, how could you enjoy dreamland while I'm still awake," I said, laughing and responding to his remark.

Bless him. Well, hopefully, he understands my character a bit, and if not, then that's his problem.

As I arrived back home, I placed his unwanted spanner in my drawer by the door and thought that he had my bowls from the last time we cooked during the winter break and he took the food home, and now I have his spanner. Tick for toe, gift exchanged. Let's see who will remember first to give each what belongs to the other. Good luck with that if he remembers first.

Almost a week had gone by and a picture was posted on our staff workgroup page that he had taken. You see, our school was celebrating the 100th day of the school. His team had got all their students to stand in the way that represents 100. I must say, it was very impressive even though I didn't reply to the messages that were streaming on my phone from other staff who were also impressed.

The following morning, on my way to school with Dani, I mentioned how impressed I was, only for her to tell me that it was nicorn-poo's idea. Well, I say, such a great idea, I thought. Let me now celebrate with him how fascinated I am with his brain. So I sent him the same 100 picture with amaze/clap emoji, quoting 'very impressive'.

Honestly, I sent it not expecting no reply back from him. To my surprise, about 30 minutes later, a message came through from him: 'Although, the 1 is a little dodgy, I'm quite happy with it', he said.

So I decided to respond since I felt happy. 'The 1 has a style of its own…makes it even more impressive. Have you been in the spirit week of dressing up?'

He then wrote, 'Of course. For the kids'.

'Nice one. Where is a picture for evidence? Not saying I don't believe you', I said, chuckling to myself.

'Hahaha, good try; you'll need to see me in person', he then wrote.

'Good one…don't be too shocked when you see me at your front door, haha', I cheekily replied.

After he replied with, 'Haha'. I just stopped responding, and besides, I needed to prepare for my teaching day ahead.

The rest of the weeks that went by, I saw him sometimes, either around school or the few times I decided to get the bus. But in these instances, instead of debating whether or not to say hello and thinking if he would ignore me, I decided to take the attitude of not caring. I purposely said hello loud and stared at him until he responded hello.

Then I carried on my way. One time, I was already on the school bus and he came on, so I tried the same thing. After he responded, he then decided to sit in front of me. Sure I poked his ears once during the bus ride and pretended it wasn't me, but I didn't even mind him for the rest of the time but carried on having a conversation with one of my guy friends who was sitting behind me.

I'm so glad we could come to an unstated mutual maturity agreement of being civil and grown-up despite the fact that feelings were probably once there…

Chapter 12

The Unexpected Ride...From Nicorn-Poo to Candy

Another weekend was about to swing from my eyes. I just don't get how time flew by. Every weekend is the same thing. Honestly, if I were ever to rule a country or be best friend with the country's government, I would make sure they establish a law for a three-day weekend. Only four days should be working days.

That indeed will be life, and I won't be surprised if that country will be flooded with people. Our motto would be, 'we care about your well-being as you cannot give what you don't have. We want to put into you too'. Who wouldn't love such a life? Only a crazy person wouldn't. No offence to them out there.

As I settled myself before bedtime, a message came through from Dani that she was not riding to work with me tomorrow as she had taken a day off. Oh, dear. Bless her. I hoped it's nothing serious. As I conversed messages with her, I had this crazy thought. Mmm, wouldn't it be funny if I ended up riding with nicorn-poo tomorrow?

I mean, I could just message him and find out if he is leaving early and just share a didi taxi with him. As the thought swamped across my mind, I wanted to slap it away—what a crazy idea. Anyway, I better sleep before my mind turns against me.

I couldn't be bothered to have him ignore my messages or be forced into it. After all, tomorrow is a new week, and I don't want it to be ruined by him spoiling my mood.

Rise and shine, I got up by the morning light grazing across my face. As I got ready for work, the crazy idea shot across my mind again. Why on earth did I think about this? Did I desire to share a ride with him?

No, of course not. I needed to stop these silly thoughts and get ready. After all, I don't want to be late for work; I had to prep for things before the students arrive.

After I finished getting ready, I decided to have breakfast and make a sandwich for my lunch, even though my first alarm to leave the house had rung. Oh well, I can't start the day on a hungry stomach. Absolutely not for the sake of the kids.

As I placed the last spoon of cereal in my mouth, the snooze alarm began to ring. Still, I didn't want to leave the dirty dishes in the sink, so I washed them before stepping out of the door, especially as I didn't like to see dirty dishes in the sink, almost like a pet peeve.

I stood there by the lift, waiting for the doors to open. I better book my didi taxi to be there when I arrive by the gate. Once again, the thought and feelings came to my mind. *What if I see him when I head downstairs?* Ugh, nicorn-poo, you're not even paying rent in my brain and you keep on having free access. So uncalled for. I hope you're happy.

The lift could not have been even more slow this morning. At last, it brought me downstairs and I was able to find a didi before I left my building door, but it was about 5 minutes away. Oh no, the rain was worse than what it seemed when I was still inside my apartment. Why did I leave my umbrella in school?

Goodness me. I should just permanently leave it in my bag. I hope my coat does justice. I don't want to be falling ill. What? How is it even possible? God, indeed you have a sense of humour. Are you kidding me? Before I could even finish walking around the corner and towards the gate, guess who I saw. Yup, you guessed correctly, nicorn-poo.

Only heaven knows how it's possible that he was also leaving this time. Before I could even finish pondering over the situation right now, my hands first turned against me as I waved and said hi. He always responded the same without hesitation.

What is my mouth doing? Without a second thought, my mouth turned against me and said, "Have you booked your taxi?"

"Yes, it's here," he said.

"Oh, good. May I come with you, please?" I responded.

"Sure. Have you not booked?" He then said.

"Yes, but it's still far away."

"No worries," he said. "However, I called the didi for the other gate, so we will have to walk there if you don't mind," he responded.

"I don't mind; it's better than nothing," I quickly said back.

As we walked to the other gate with my hood up, he had his umbrella and placed it on himself and me.

Without warning, he started talking away. "How was your weekend?" he said, "Did you get up to much?" So after explaining my weekend to him, it's only fair I find out about his.

"I went away with friends and did a bit of sightseeing…" and without warning, he was speaking like an erupted volcano.

"What?" I screeched. "You're such a daredevil. And where was my invite to the Great Wall."

"Sorry, how could I have forgotten your invite? But I didn't end up seeing the Great Wall…" he said.

"Okay, I forgive you," I jokily said back. "Just don't do it again, having fun without me."

"Of course not…" Then he started talking about the process being smooth and so forth.

As we approached the didi, he opened the door for me to enter the back. I entered and was about to close the door behind me, then guess who was also making his way to the back too? Of course him. As we sat next to each other at the back of the didi, the conversation became endless.

From one topic to the other, he was talking like a house on fire, this time asking questions and initiating and steering the conversation. This guy left me speechless. Is this still the same guy, asking me about my summer plans, upcoming Labour holiday plans, the birthday celebration of Sammy next week, work, and sharing things of himself that I didn't even ask the questions to.

Where is the news reporter when I need them to capture this moment? Only heaven knows if it will ever recur again. I know for sure I'm not betting my breath on it. The whole time, my heart began to melt once again as we smiled at each other in endless conversation.

If only this car journey could last forever. I mean, do we really need to go to work. Let's be daredevils together and drive around the city. I'm sure the school will survive one day without us. I know my little ones will, but only heaven knows if his would.

The didi halt at the school gate as these thoughts race through my mind. I sighed internally, silently praying the car would just quickly take off again before we could get out. In fact, this driver should kidnap us.

Without a moment too soon, he opened the door and stepped out of the vehicle standing by the door and holding the umbrella for me to step out under it. Pushing my disappointment back, I followed him out to realise he had placed the umbrella over me so I won't get wet. Stepping out of the car, he then closed the door behind me.

The conversation continued between us as we made our way to the security by the entrance gate. After checking health codes, we both made our way through the body temperature walk-through. Oh no. I then realised we were in two separate buildings opposite to each other. For me, the main entrance was a turn to the right, and he had to go straight ahead then turn left.

Now we had to part ways and I was going to get wet. Actually, I quickly thought to myself, why don't I be cheeky and ask him to walk me to my entrance door, even though it was out of his way. Still, it's not the first time I was being cheeky. He should know me by now, I think. So with no hesitation, I asked him, "Is it too much for me to ask you to drop me at my entrance?"

"Of course not," he replied. And away we went as he walked me to the entrance.

As we got there, I thanked him and we said our goodbyes. "Have a good day."

"You as well, have a good one." Then we parted ways. As I strolled to my classroom, I pondered and replayed what had just happened. *Was it a dream, a fragment of my imagination, or the silver lining which was finally being unfolded?* Only heaven knows once again.

Now toned down on the smiling from east to west, I told myself, I had a long day ahead of me and needed a clear mind.

A couple of days passed, and I arrived early at school again. Not long after, while still preparing for the day ahead, the announcement speakers in my classroom room began to crackle and echo something. *Oh, it's the senior director speaking. I wonder what's so important she's announcing.*

"Good morning, teachers…sorry for the not-so-clear start to my announcement. As you're aware, the school has been raising funds for growing more trees and looking after our environment. I want to let you know which class has raised the most money and appreciate their hard effort; they will be receiving a pizza party.

"The class is in grade 2…congratulations, everyone, but the winner is 2A. We will be contacting you shortly to discuss your well-earned pizza party."

Mmm, I thought. *I wonder who 2A is. Why do I have a feeling that's nicorn's class? But maybe I could be wrong since, after all, there are four teachers in total in that grade. Maybe it's Dani's class. Well, whoever it is, I wish they could be generous and share the pizza party with me. You know what, I'm going to message nicorn and find out if that's his class.*

'Are you 2A?', the message went off to him.

'Yes!'

'You must know why I'm messaging you?', I said.

'You heard the announcement', he replied with smirks emojis.

'Let's just say, you're OFFICIALLY my new best friend, no argument…', I said with a chuckle emoji.

'Wow, that's going to be my new Instagram bio. Officially Sarah's best friend'.

'You're on Insta…and how come you haven't got your best friend, aka me, on there? I welcome it. So best friend, don't forget I need special treatment above your other friends', I replied.

'Hahaha, if you're interested in me offering you a pizza slice, I may be able to do that. But that's about it', he replied.

'#AistheBestFriendEVER. That's my quote for today's journal', I wrote back with a laughing face.

'Haha, that's a good quote', he replied.

Okay, Sarah, no more flirting, I told myself. Even though I didn't have a clue that I was doing it. The things our stomach can make us do without even realising it. Oh well. But one thing I can say, nicorn is beginning to prove himself with the heart I always knew he had.

I mean, after all, no one is perfect, and who has made me the judge of the land to be judging his weaknesses. But I can consider his heart is good in wanting to help others. So nicorn, you've redeemed yourself from nicorn-poo to candy.

Although, you can come in different types to others, you're surely sweet to have around.

Chapter 13
The Ride Continues...

What a weekend. I spent my Saturday working most of the day for entrance exams at school and then I went to two birthday celebrations since I didn't want to let my colleagues down. I'm glad today is Sunday, and I decided to camp out at home. No one should call me for any emergency because I surely won't answer. They better call the police as there is more hope for them to answer than me.

After catching up with my mom, friends back home, and the States, I started to feel peckish. Maybe I should make some pancakes. I wonder what candy is up to. Perhaps I should invite him to have some or we can make it together. But then again, is that a good idea.

Well, I contemplated; we are friends now. I don't know how it happened but friendship is undoubtedly there. He even liked my moment post earlier. Okay, instead of debating this, I would just send him a message. If he doesn't want to come then he would just say no. After all, I'm not putting a gun to his head to say yes.

Once again, a message went out to him. When he sees my name pops on his phone, I wonder what he thinks. Oh well.

I'm sure one day I will find out. Till then, pancakes are on the line.

'If you need a break, pop over for a bit, lol', I wrote to him.

'Haha, what you up to', he replied.

'Pancakes', I said.

'I wish! But I'm not home ATM'.

'Unlucky, lol. If you decide not to come too late, still pop round', I cheekily said back.

Then I went off to make and enjoy pancakes. Why should my tummy suffer because he is not home? That's if it's true. I'm not saying I don't believe him, especially as we are now on a new leaf—still, no comment.

A couple of days went by, and it's back to Sunday again. Once again, I'm back at work to make up for the Labour holiday. As much as I love this country, I don't think I will ever understand the holiday system. How can you tell me you're giving me a holiday but only to tell me, I need to work on some of my weekends to make up for it.

To be honest, I don't even think I should try to understand it before it might hurt my brain. After all, I should stick to my favourite quote of 'when in Rome, do as the Romans do'. Even though I'm far from Rome.

As Dani and I stood to wait by the gate for the didi taxi, guess who came round the corner. Yes, the one and only, candy. "Have you guys called the didi?" he said.

"Yeah, we have."

"Do you mind if I come with you guys?" he said quickly after I responded.

"Of course, you can. I mean, I can put you on top of the roof. That's the least I could do for you," I said, chuckling to myself. Which also made him smile and giggle.

I was sincerely shocked. Usually, he got his own didi. There was even a time (way before) Dani told me she had asked him at work to ride with us but he preferred to ride by himself since he is not a morning person (well, at least that's what she said). I don't know how much of it is true, to be honest.

During the didi ride, I ensured there was no moment of silence. Away I went with my mouth like a waterfall. Asking questions, responding to him, and making sure he enjoyed being in our presence of this didi. After all, he might change his mind on his lonely perspective of riding didi. That's if this candy is not a tough one to crack.

As the ride went on, he asked me how I spent yesterday since it was our only day off. So away I went with my detail talking but this time, I quickly skimmed through my physical therapy appointment since not many knew about my back. But to my surprise, this candy was listening. After I finished talking, he then said, "How come you went to the physical therapy appointment?"

So I explained about my back and then he asked another question about what I described. Seriously, I was surprised. He sounded so caring and concerned. Wow, he indeed wanted to be eye candy again. But nope. The iceberg has not yet melted. You are candy and should be thankful for that.

In no time, we arrived again at work. What is wrong with these didi taxi drivers? The time I want them to be driving slow, that's when they are speeding faster than a cheetah.

Why are they against these breathless moments which have been captured for eternity?

I bet the times I want them to drive fast, that's when a snail will be faster than them. I hope they are happy because I'm not.

After going through security at the gate and temperature check, I said goodbye to them both (since they were both going to the same building). As I began to walk off, he then echoed out, "Have a good day." And off we parted ways again. Only time will tell if these moments are just one of or a paintbrush stroke for a beautiful picture still being painted by the artist.

Chapter 14
The Favour: Who Would Have Guessed?

Honestly, graduation needs to hurry up. For the last several weeks, it has been the constant talk, and it was summarised into the words, 'It needs to be BIG'. After watching the previous years, I've been deflated already. But I'm not allowed to.

For the sake of my students, those 25 minions needed me to keep going, and for their sake, I would give them the best graduation experience. It honestly hadn't even been 3 weeks since we had the International Day's celebration, and need I say, that was extremely big with the capital B.

One of the management held our first meeting for the International Day before we even started planning and quoted the words, 'Think Big, Think Museum'. And need I say, that was precisely what happened. In the beginning, most of the new teachers doubted and could only see the problem of it coming altogether, and I confess, I was one of the chief doubters of the logistics. But, I was soon proven wrong.

I love when that happens sometimes. It surely reminds me how much of a human being I am. Anyway, the International

Day took place and I even purposely visited candy's classroom to see how he had showcased his country. Also, cheeky me, I requested his class performance even though they had previously performed to others just before my students and I walked into his classroom.

Still, my heart fluttered and I smiled when he adhered to my request because it showed either of these two things. One, he wanted to show off how awesome his class was and their hard work, or he hears me and if he could make me smile in any way, then he would. Only heaven and he know if any of the statements are true or it's just a figment of my imagination.

Anyway, fast-forward to graduation. It was literally less than a week and it had been so hectic to organise while reflecting on the whole process. From the costumes to the music, the decorations and last but not the least, since it was one of the main things, the dance which I had to teach my students. Mind you, I'm not the best dancer or even a dancer, but I do love dancing, although it's mainly not in the rhythm.

In the midst of all this graduation preparation, I was quite stressed out. About two and a half weeks ago, my mom and cousin sent me a package from the U.K., but it was still stuck in customs as they were giving me a headache for clearing it. I had been in backward and forward conversation with one of the customs clearance officers and he was a pain in the butt.

Literally, I supplied lots of evidence of whatever he asked for but each time, he thought of new things to frustrate me with. My family paid a lot for this package to be sent here and this was the headache I'm receiving. Honestly, sometimes I wish I knew or was close to someone in higher authority like the government.

I feel like some unnecessary situations in my life won't even happen then. The most frustrating part was that I needed my prescribed medications in the package with the prescription letter from my doctor. Ugh, only God could help me.

A day went by, and I attended a friend's surprise birthday party. While there, it just so happened candy's team leader was there, and she and I happened to converse. Hold and behold, his name came up and she let it slip to me that he was leaving work early before the end of the academic year as he was going to the U.K. since a family member was ill.

Honestly, I just wanted to find where he was and give him a big hug at that moment. I know most men are not inclined to their emotions, but when hearing such news, all I can think of is wanting to be there for him. But the question is, how do I? The funniest thing is he had mentioned to me months back that he might go back to the U.K. this summer, but the reason why he was going he had left out of the conversation.

And honestly, I understand. All I could do was whisper a little prayer for him during that moment. In the midst of that, an idea popped into my mind. I mean, it literally popped and it seemed crazy at first, and I didn't know how I would even approach him to ask. So, since it seemed an insensitive idea, I kicked it away from my mind.

The following day, I decided to get the bus home on time and not stay late again at school. Walking to the bus with Dani, I happened to see candy standing far off on a phone call. He smiled as we walked past and I gave a gentle wave. I was sipping on my refreshing drink while getting on the bus, and the idea of what I wanted to ask him once again came to my mind.

But no, I couldn't, and I wouldn't. We were not even that close for me to ask him such things. Still, the idea wouldn't budge from my mind and heart. *Ugh, why me.*

I sat at the back, across from Dee, as she was already on the bus, and we began to catch up. Not long after, candy came on the bus from the first door and talked to someone there. But for some strange reason, I had this deep sense that he was going to sit in the seat in front of mine. I almost chuckled with my drink at that idea.

I mean, why he would want to when there were plenty of available seats before mine. So I decided not to notice he had got on the bus as I continued to sip my drink and converse away with Dee. Within a couple of minutes, I could catch a glimpse of someone walking in my direction.

Hold and behold, candy approached our direction. "Where is my drink?" He cheekily opened his mouth and said to me.

"I'm drinking it for us," I cheekily replied as I laughed.

"Wow, how could you not be sharing. Very insensitive," he then responded as he sat in the seat in front of me and laughed. At this moment, I was speechless. Not because of what he said but because he was sitting in front of me as I had felt. Wow, that was weird.

Soon after that, the bus took off, and the idea once again came to mind for me to ask. No, I refused. As I was warring within me, hold and behold, my hand and mouth went against me. My hand reached out and almost stroked the back of his shoulder. With no hesitation, he turned around and said, "What's up?"

"Hey, I need to talk to you about something important but not here," I burst out.

"Oh no, what is it? What's important?" He promptly responded back, wanting to know.

"No," I quickly responded. "You don't need to worry. I need to talk to you about something important and ask you something, but you don't need to worry," I replied, trying to calm his anxious mind down.

"What?" he said back. "Is that all you're saying? I want to know. Or I will say no now," he said, laughing.

"What, no way," I said, laughing back. "No, you can't, and don't worry, it's nothing terrible. I will come and find you if that's okay?"

"Yes, that's fine," he replied.

"Thanks. Don't worry; it's nothing bad," I repeated with a smile.

Not long after, the bus came to a stop. Candy quickly got off and back on a phone call. He shot off from the bus as fast as lightning and walked off. Whatever it was, it seemed important. I would find him later as I was going to spend some time with my friend, Carol, today.

We were going for dinner and movies—my first time going to the movies here, so I was excited. I aimed to be back home by 8, so I could go and see candy before he hit the hay by 8:30. He's worse than I am when it comes to sleeping early. I tend to sleep quite early but I challenge myself to stay awake at times.

Strolling from the bus stop, I had to quickly pop home to drop my things before I went and met Carol. As I walked through the entrance gates of the compound area, I saw him again but talking to one of our colleagues. After smiling and quickly conversing with that colleague, I then said to him I would come and find him later on. “Okay, no worries,” he replied.

Well, let’s just say, it was gone past bedtime by the time I came back home after spending time with Carol. It was so late that I was extremely exhausted. So coming to find him was out of the window because I knew he would be fast asleep with the fairies.

The following day after work, I picked up my packages nearby and decided to go to his building. Funny enough, I had no clue if he was home or not, so I just took a chance. In the lift, my heart pounded. Mmm, I wonder. Maybe I should have messaged to see if he was home.

But then again, this was not the first time showing up at his front door unexpectedly. As these thoughts processed in my mind, I stood in front of his front door for a minute. Then hesitating, I walked away from his door and back into the lift without even knocking to see if he was home. Was it consciousness or craziness that kicked in? I will never know.

So walking back home to my building with my many packages and umbrella over my head, trying not to get wet, I began to question what had just happened. Only heaven knew, and I’m grateful he didn’t open his door as I was walking away from it. That would have left my tongue tangled.

Arriving in my building, I decided to message him because I had not reached out to say I was no longer coming the day before. I was feeling bad. I hoped he didn’t think I’m rude. It wasn’t possible to message back then. So here I went and sent him a message.

‘Hey, you free for me to pop for 5 mins?’

Then the wait began because we knew this guy was against replying to my messages straight away or an antiphone person, and he's allergic to being near his phone. Whichever one it is, I don't think I will ever know. It might just be one of those mysteries that I would need a top investigator to solve for me. But that idleness is not my portion, so it will not happen anytime soon.

About 25 minutes later, when I had almost forgotten about the message I had sent, a message came through from him.

'Yeah, come through'.

Without hesitation, I sent him another message that I would see him soon, and away I left my apartment and strolled along to his, and this time, made sure I knocked and waited at his front door.

Without a moment to spare, he opened the door with a smile. "Come through," he uttered, and without hesitation, I stepped in, taking off my shoes and closing the door behind me. I stood there for a second, complaining about my Taobao orders since, once again, they had screwed up the items I ordered.

Slightly interrupting me, he asked me to take a seat on the sofa and went out into his balcony to pick up his laundry since it began to rain more heavily. Upon arriving back inside, he asked me how my day was, and there the invitation was for me to open my mouth and let it run like water on how my day was.

Then after, the same question was posed to him, and need I say, his mouth was a tap that dripped considerately. Then, we conversed more on how work has been, the upcoming graduation for my students, and many other things. After venting off my Taobao crises to him and showing sympathy to me, I finally kicked into why I was indeed there. At this moment, the anticipation was beginning to make him anxious.

Without another moment to spare, I dug into it. "So you know you are off to the U.K. next week?"

"Huh?" He replied. "How do you know I was going?"

"Well," I said, "remember you mentioned months back that you might be going?"

"Yes," he said. "But nothing was definite till less than 2 weeks ago."

"Well, I assume you still were." I quickly jumped into what he said while skipping the part his team lead confirmed and let it slip to me.

"Oh," he replied. "Okay." Then he mentioned trying to sort out his other passport as he was going to use that to travel instead, since he has two, so there will be no complications of him coming back into the country. But he was waiting till next week and it should be ready.

So I carried on. "You know I'm on prescribed medication…" Away I went, running my mouth once again as I narrated everything under the sun just to build the story for him. But the beautiful thing about this was that he was constantly chirping in and out during the process.

Finally, I got to the actual point of 'The Favour'. "Well, the thing is, may you help me bring some items please, including the other items from the package which were posted but wouldn't clear customs here as it was above the personal gift item limit. The items included my prescribed medications and perfumes I love."

I told him how I had enough until the end of this month of what the doctor had given me (from the last time I was previously leaving the U.K. and I thought I would be returning home for summer but didn't know COVID still be around to prevent that). I went on and became very vulnerable to him about personal things to do with my health that I hadn't intended on sharing, but it was so natural to speak to him without any judgment in his eyes.

He looked at me and attentively listened as I spoke, which meant more than he knew. I don't usually open up so deeply with everyone but only those I truly trust and are dear to me. He should indeed count himself lucky. Before I could finish talking, he quickly said, "Of course, I can do that for you. It's not a big thing and won't be a problem at all."

Wow, I was speechless at this moment. It meant more to me than he would ever know. Throughout the time at his home, we carried on talking; we joked about him taking a risk for me; how he should do hard labour when he goes to his aunt's place in the U.K.; how he should just empty his luggage just to bring my things back.

Also, we joked about how not to be caught at the airport when they asked him did he pack all his baggage by himself, and he should reply no, there was a lady who placed all her things in it (referring to me with a laugh). I responded, "Well if you get in trouble for me, I might come and visit you sometimes," with a laugh.

In between the conversation, he showed his concerns about whether I would be okay until the newly prescribed medication came and what I would do regarding my annual blood check-up. My heart felt lighter and lighter as the conversation went on, knowing he was genuine. He later said that once he received his aunt's address, he would forward it to give it to my cousin to post the items to him.

Not long after, I said I wouldn't steal any more of his time as I prepared my way to leave his flat. I stood up once again and expressed how thankful I was, and without hesitation, I went towards him and hugged him. It came as unexpected to both of us, but I still did it anyway, with him hugging me back.

Walking out the door as I said goodbye to him, a bigger smile shone brightly across my face like a newer leaf might have been established between us. But once again, only heaven knows. All I could think of was so much for popping over for just 5 mins. More like 40 minutes. Who would have guessed he would be so willing to agree to this favour. He sure was full of surprises.

Finally, graduation came and my students looked dazzling with their costumes and dashing as they performed. I decided to send him a message asking if his passport was all sorted. And once again, his allergy reaction had begun with not replying to me. A day went past, and he then responded, saying yes and sharing his aunt's U.K. address with me, asking me not to share it out to no one else.

With a promise, I said I won't, even though I was soon going to share with my cousin who would be posting my packages to him. Within a couple of days, he was about to leave for the U.K., he didn't tell me the exact time but no offence was taken.

I knew it was either the night or early hours of that morning. That didn't stop me from sending him a message, even though most probably he won't be replying. Still, I wanted him to know I was thinking of his travels.

'Wishing you journey mercies tonight/tomorrow. Enjoy the UK', I sent him.

Like an annoying fly who passed you by, so did my message quickly went to him, with no felony taken if he was to reply or not.

Two days went by and I woke up to his message.

‘Appreciate it! Have a great summer’.

Well, he didn’t have to reply but glad he did. In the midst of my amazement, I decided to text back with a chuckle cheekily.

‘Thanks. Try not to miss us too much’.

And there it was. Like a cricket, no reply came back from him. Still, I didn’t regret sending out my quirky message. Even though he hadn’t replied, I hoped it made him at least chuckle on the inside.

As the week went by, I passed his aunt’s address and number to my cousin and asked her to post all my packages.

Once again, I woke up to his message.

‘Hey! Did you send the package up to the UK yet?’

Mmm, it was impressive how he could ignore the previous message and start on a new branch. It was a skill I hoped to learn from him one day. In fact, he should teach a class on it. I’m sure people like me would benefit significantly from it.

After contacting my cousin, I responded not long after to his message.

‘Morning, my cousin is sending it today to your aunt’s address. Sorry, she has been waiting for the other package which was stuck in customs, but she received it yesterday’.

And that was that. No reply back from him, but I would not expect it any other way. That’s just him and his make-up, and I had to just embrace it all.

Later that evening, I caught up with my cousin again but only to find out she hadn’t yet posted the package because the other one stuck in customs won’t be arriving until three days later. She received the wrong information. Only after three days would she post all the items.

Well, I should either contact candy to explain that the things have not been posted and I got it wrong, or follow his example and keep quiet as a cricket. After a long debate, I decided for once to follow in his example and see if I was also born to walk in his style too. Till then, we just had to wait and see.

Chapter 15
The Phone Call: Four-Way Conversation...

Now DHL has strictly used all the grace I had for them. I don't know who to pin the blame on, the customs or the DHL Company. I was sitting on the plane, ready for my flight to en-route to Kunming, then my phone began to ring. It was my cousin to give me the latest update. I salute her at this point in time because I would have given up if I were in her shoe.

The other day, she called for a quick catch-up since it was her birthday, after all. Quick as in 40 minutes. As I picked up her call, she had excitement with some quirk in her voice. So, she has been waiting for over three days now and still, no sign of the parcel.

She decided to call candy's aunt's number to speak to him and update him since I had previously given her the go-ahead. This phone call was much of catch-up on how she had been spending her birthday and revealing the juicy details of what had happened when she had called the aunt earlier on that day. And the conversation went like this…

Phone: ring, ring, ring…

Candy's aunt: "Hello, who's this?"

Cousin: "Hello, this is…a friend from China, cousin. May I please speak to…?"

Candy's aunt: "Okay, hold on a minute…" (She then went to where he was, handing over her phone to him) "It's for you."

Cousin: "Hello…This is Sarah's cousin."

Candy: "Oh hi…"

And just like that, the conversation went on between them like long lost acquaintance whose path had just crossed again.

Well, let's just say my cousin couldn't help herself but narrate the whole conversation to me. I could not stop laughing. This guy must think I'm a nutter or even why he had agreed in the first place to do this favour for me, especially after this four-way conversation he had just experienced.

Only heaven knows what he has been thinking since that phone call or, even worse, what conversation was conversed between him and his aunt about this whole situation. Look at what DHL and the customs have led me to do. I was truly lost for words. So here I was on the plane reflecting on my cousin, and I's previous phone call and embracing myself to receive the new news.

After explaining the current update to me, I was even too tired to speak concerning this. How could DHL now be telling her the package was still in China customs (it hadn't been sent), and the message she had received from them last week was a mistake. They themselves do not understand why the package was still in customs.

If they don't understand, how on earth would we. So with a deep sigh and frustration, I then told my cousin just to send the other things she had with her to candy without the package items which were still in customs. If she doesn't hear back from DHL properly (before the end of the day on her side), she should go ahead. I'm tired of this whole thing and it had been about almost two months of backward and forward with DHL.

They could just compensate because I don't know what job they are doing. It was undoubtedly not a job I want to be part of. Without saying further, she agreed to post the other items tomorrow for next day delivery so candy can receive them. How would I even look him in the face after what I was putting him through because of my packages?

All I can say that he was surely a keeper from my side but just doesn't know it yet. Only time will tell if this truth will be revealed to him. Till then, let's hope he found this whole experience of agreeing to do this favour as funny as I did, even though no one is currently laughing.

Chapter 16
Confusion: The Cricket Is Back in Business

To say I love summer break is an understatement. I'm sincerely loving the whole experience of being in Yunnan with Carol, and it has been a tremendous blast so far. We flew here the following day after school broke up. I have honestly been having such a wonderful time and it's hard to believe it will soon be over.

Nevertheless, I will be venturing off on my next adventures (after all, I had planned to be ambitious this holiday since I can't go home to see my family and friends).

I decided to reach out to candy during this time away as he kept creeping up on my mind a lot. But then again, after the previous conversation between my cousin and candy, everything was becoming so unreal to me. Making sense of everything was beyond what my mind could contain during this restful holiday.

But candy did tell my cousin I should reach out and text him. This baffled me more, especially as he has been a cricket to the last message I sent.

On the other hand, what could I do? I needed my things. So like an idle person, which I'm so not, I decided to reach out to him once again.

'Hiya, I hope your holiday is going well, and you're enjoying the scenery and hospitality…My cousin told me she posted the items to you; I just wanted to find out if you received them. She posted it in your aunt's name. The parcel is a brown box'.

Well, that's that. I've sent the message and now the waiting begins.

A day went past, and still nothing from him. Then another day. It was like he had gone back into the business of cricketing; not a sound from him. I really wondered what goes through his mind sometimes. Actually, not even sometimes but most of the time. I mean even a lot of the time.

Was he not the one that told my cousin for me to message him? Why then must he not respond? Before my thoughts could take a toll on me, hold and behold, the cricket has emerged from the underground.

'Hey! Sorry, I haven't even opened WeChat in a few weeks. I got your package yesterday; although, I'm stuck in the U.K. as there has been a travel ban, I'll give it to you when I get back'.

Now that message left me flabbergasted and feeling bad. Oh, man. I wish there was something I could do. I don't want him to be stuck out of the country. Things or none, I still wanted him here safe and sound. Yes, there were questions in my mind about him not being able to open his WeChat in a few weeks (I'm not saying I don't believe him).

Anyway, my heart felt terrible. I might not fully know what was going on with him, but I still felt compassionate. So humbling myself once again, I decided to reply. Forgetting to take offence at the way he had been to me. Forgiving and forgetting are things I've been practicing, especially when it came to him.

'How come you didn't open WeChat for a while? Is everything okay? I'm sorry that you're currently stuck in the U.K. Is there anything you would like me to do for you in the meantime?' I decided to message back.

Well, even though I had no right to pry into his business and ask him such personal questions, but I cared because I'm concerned. He can interpret it the way he wanted. I won't take offence to it.

Here we go, as a ghost once again, silence arose, and he was back into the entire cricketing business. But I told myself I wasn't going to let it annoy me. After all, I was having a lovely holiday in Nantong currently, and would be heading to Beijing next.

Two days went by, and I spoke to my cousin, who told me the other package (that was stuck in customs) finally arrived. She posted my prescribed medicine with the doctor's consent and business letters from the company I was involved with to candy's aunt's address. I also gave her the go-ahead to send them, even though I haven't heard from candy since the previous message.

I'm sure it will be fine. After all, he was still in the country and I hoped and prayed that he was still put at his aunt's place. I'm not saying he should spend his whole summer there, but…let's leave that to linger. I decided once again, since it was becoming more accustomed to me, to reach out first and let him know about the other package coming his way, as it had been sent the next day delivery.

‘Hey, sorry for disturbing you. I just wanted to let you know that my cousin posted the other few items that were stuck previously in customs. It should be with you by tomorrow. Thank you once again!’

After the message was sent, I felt funny inside and not in a ha-ha way. Why did I feel bad all of a sudden for sending him a message? Was it because he kept ignoring my messages for a while (and sometimes forever), or was it because I gave the go-ahead to my cousin to send this new package in his name without finding out his whereabouts or seeing if he was still okay with him.

Either way, I wasn’t expecting a reply from him anytime soon, so there was no need for me to worry; after all, I was off to the Great Wall tomorrow.

Morning came, and the journey began for the Great Wall. So far, I absolutely loved my time in Beijing, which was funny as I am not a city person. But for once, I was beginning to reconsider. If the opportunity ever arises, I won’t mind moving to Beijing.

Tee and her friends think I’m bizarre for saying that. Maybe it’s true; maybe it’s not. Who truly knows? In a way, you could say I preferred it more than Shanghai, but I’m not one to go and declare it on the mountain tops.

The whole day was spent on the Great Wall with Tee and her friends, and I must say, the way I felt being on there and overlooking phenomenal views, my eyes were blessed and privileged to be experiencing such a truly remarkable wonder of the world. It really inspired me to see and experience the rest of the wonders of the world.

As I was coming down with the others from the Great Wall, feeling on top of the world and waiting for the bus to drive us back to the city centre, messages came from candy. All of a sudden, my heart began to thump loudly. I mean, I was so used to him not replying to my messages and being a cricket that I don't know how to handle it when he resumes from that.

Right now, I was on a high point after what I have experienced and nothing can bring me down. I went on to the message without a moment to spare.

'Hey! I got your package, one with medicine and perfume in it.'

'All good.'

'I've already left my aunt's place. and I'm in London now.'

'However, Sarah, my aunt is telling me it's illegal for me to bring it into the transit country (where I'm heading next) and I'll get done for it if they find it on me. I'm a little concerned about bringing the medicine over, to be honest'.

Tears began to build up in my eyes. What's the matter with this guy? We already discussed this when he was still in here and he was the one more than willing to do this favour for me. I didn't put a gun to his head, did I? I was honestly angry now. And that was it. I responded in my emotional state without thinking, tears streaming from my face.

'Hi, thanks for getting back to me. You can just throw the medicine away and I will sort them out here. Thanks anyway'.

How could I allow myself to be in this state after my lovely experience on the Great Wall? It was not fair. I should know better, and I do know better, but why do my emotions not understand better? I called my cousin after and vented off in tears. After patiently listening to me and comforting me, I felt better.

My cousin said she had left a voicemail on his aunt's phone, informing her of the new package and what was in it for her to pass it on to him. I couldn't help but sigh deeply. I think most frustrating part is not really my medicine, as I could sort them out with my new doctor here after I returned from my adventures.

And, of course, I didn't want him to ever get in trouble for me with the authorities. You don't joke with people like that and I understand and respect why the laws are in place. I was also not even upset because his aunt doesn't like me (since I feel she doesn't). But I was upset because of his lack of communication.

It sincerely frustrated me to the core of my bones. If he had just been consistent in replying straight away when I reached out, the situation wouldn't have come to this matter. I'm not saying he should have dropped everything he was doing or had going on there to respond to me, but at least be a bit consistent in replying. That's all I desired.

Was it too much expectation from one person? And to make matters even worse, my letters (including my business ones for the company) were in the package which was now sitting in his aunt's place. Now that he was in London and no longer in Wales, how would I receive them? Does it mean it will stay with his aunt forever?

Personal information for the business was on the letters and I didn't want it to get into the wrong hands. I didn't know what to do and it was not like he would reach out with a consoling message after mine or give me an alternative. I don't know what he wanted me to reply to his message but I sure know I gave a different reply from what he could have expected.

Besides, if I had responded with 'you should…', would he have cared?

Why me? How did I ever get myself in this mess? Once I get the perfumes from him upon his return, I was going to give him a piece of my mind and tell him to delete me from his life and phone. This I cannot handle or take anymore. Once again, this had reminded me why I shouldn't have bothered in the first place.

After all this whirlwind of thoughts, the bus was finally ready to leave for the city. I got on the bus and made my way to the back seat with the others. Laying my head on the glass window, I settled my mind as I drifted away to relaxation.

Anyway, I thought to myself, *Why should I allow my lovely summer adventures to be halted by someone who didn't seem to care about my feelings?* Sooner or later, as sleep was knocking on my eyelids, the thoughts lingered in my mind; the unexpected journey I thought candy and I were once on, was now brought to light that we were merely strangers passing by each other.

Chapter 17
This Is It: The Crossroad...

What a morning. Honestly, this professional development needed to finish. Some of them have been so random and felt like it was just to keep us, teachers, busy and occupied even though we have little time to ourselves. Speaking of that, they have given us a stack of tasks to complete but with no time at all.

A miracle is what they are expecting us to do before the students finally resumed, and with little time as well. Once again, I was in school early and tried to remain focused, especially after waking up to see messages from the unexpected. Not directly to me but the messages were on the group page with all the teachers who lived at our location and the property management.

He had arrived late last night at his apartment but his key card wasn't working, and he needed the management to help get him in. But why do I care, especially as I had not heard from him the rest of the summer. Not after the Great Wall blew up. My mind had to focus today, especially since we had the first professional development together.

I was in my classroom and decided to head to the room where the training was early to find the perfect seat for my team and me. As I walked forward and turned slightly, only to notice a figure I couldn't forget in the far distance. Heart pounding and racing, I quickened my steps to the training room. "Breathe, Sarah, Breathe," I kept on telling myself as I paced around the room with sweaty hands.

Not thinking straight, I left that room and went back into my classroom with tears filling my eyes. *Why am I so emotional? What's the matter with me?* Right, I better get myself together before anyone sees me and think the overwhelmedness of the professional developments is getting to me.

Off I went again into the training room, but this time, the teachers crowded everywhere as I opened the doors which left me feeling nauseous. Quickly, I made my way to where my team was seated, only to be distracted by the presence of the one I was trying not to make eye contact with as he also walked into the room.

In the midst of this whirlwind of recollection of thoughts, I kicked my water bottle which spilled my drink everywhere around me. So much for not wanting to cause a scene for myself. Let's just say the plan of action failed as everyone's eyes zoomed on me.

Even the look of whom I was so desperately trying to avoid. Quickly, I jumped up and made my way to the bathroom to get some tissues and clean up my mess without making no eye contact with him.

"Right," I told myself as I walked away, "you've got this." Only heaven knows once again what 'you've got this' looked like.

After finally cleaning up my mess and sitting back down, I whispered a little prayer for this training to be the fastest one out of all of them. I was trying my best to fix my eyes ahead because to my side (just four seats away), there he was, sitting like there was no tomorrow.

Half of the training was completed and I couldn't be more relieved. Now we were all asked by the trainer to get up and change seats. So trying to be clever with my team, we decided to just move one place forward within the inner seats. And besides, it was too early to think of a logical chair to sit down on when we didn't even know the next task.

As I sat down, I gently turned aside only to be haunted by what I dreaded so dearly. You know who had decided to sit the next seat behind me. *What?* I thought to myself. Now I know my thoughts have betrayed me and have sided with him. Right, all I have to do is look straight ahead and whatever I do, don't look back. I mean, how hard can that be.

I wish I had not asked. Because within less than 10 seconds of thinking that, the trainer then gave us a task to turn around and speak to the person behind us and ask them some questions she had prompted us with. Now how oblivious would it be if I suddenly got up and changed seats?

Well, better now or never, I told myself as I made the 180-degree turn.

To my surprise, someone then sat next to me and I turned around eagerly, saying to him, "I guess you're my partner." A big sigh came over me as I was now left with another woman who just happened to also sit next to him behind me. Wow, what a turn of events. Thank goodness for it.

After the training, I quickly leaped out of my chair and made my way through the exit and into the safe hideout of my classroom.

The rest of the day was a blur to me. From classroom set up, to team meeting, to like I said before, anything to keep us teachers busy and exhausted. As the school day was finishing, I knew I would have to stay behind again to catch up on other tasks.

In my classroom, I was flapping around on what tasks I should execute first, and then as I lifted my head, hold and behold, my eyes locked with his. I just don't know how it happened just at that moment in time. Fate had to make him walk past my classroom, which happened to be glassed around.

When being in my classroom, I sometimes forgot the idea of not being found by anyone. Now what happened next, I seriously could not put my mind to it. My hands betrayed me once again with no warning. Then again, so did his. There my hands were waving at him and his hands were also waving at me.

To put the icing on the cake, the unexpected happened. My hands then signalled him to come to me. Like I said, up to this point, my brain was still trying to catch up with everything that had just been happening. To my surprise, he then turned around to enter the building for my classroom.

No way was this happening. Was I seriously ready for this? How is it possible all of this was happening? My heart was pounding out of my chest and my brain was trying to speed up to the current reality.

It's a shame I didn't have the chance to check if there was anything on my face, no leftover food stuck on my teeth, was

I still smelling like a decent human being. In no time, the figure appeared through my door.

As we walked towards each other, both saying hello to the other, we opened our arms and hugged tightly. Not planned, not expected but naturally just happened.

I said, "Welcome back."

Candy replied, "Thank you. How have you been?"

"I have been good, thanks. How was the summer travel?" I asked.

And from there, the conversations became endless again as nothing had ever happened to stop us from talking. In no time, 15 minutes had gone past with conversations and smiles being passed on from one another.

After some time, we were interrupted by another colleague who couldn't read the hint from us that three was a crowd. Either way, we both knew whatever had happened didn't matter. At this precise moment in time, being in the now was what we both desired.

Without a moment too soon, we both said our goodbyes, smiled and waved as he walked away. I was trying to collect my thoughts on what had just happened. The whole experience seemed like a dream that should be consider Deja vu.

Once again, we found ourselves not with a definite answer but caught in the midst of this is now, not knowing when or how our paths would cross again and what unexpected matters would our hearts unfold…

Milton Keynes UK
Ingram Content Group UK Ltd.
UKHW050722291123
433366UK00019B/283

9 781035 823499